Team Niklas

A Saints team novel

By Ally Adams

Atlas Productions

Team Niklas
First published in 2015. Reprinted 2017, 2020 and 2021.
Copyright © Ally Adams and Helen Goltz

Atlas Productions
Greenslopes QLD 4102
Web: www.atlasproductions.com.au

A catalogue record for this book is available from the National Library of Australia

*Dedicated to the office girls from the Bears.
What good times!*

Books by Ally Adams

The Saints Team series:

Team Lucas

Team Tomás

Team Niklas

Team Alex

Chapter 1

'Stop moving or I'll accidentally put it in the wrong place,' I ordered Nik. You would think a guy who had done military conscription at home in Berlin, and stood at attention for long periods of time in all sorts of weather, could stand still for a few minutes.

'Sah-sha, is it even possible to put it in the wrong place?' he asked, with a raised eyebrow.

I couldn't help but smile – the way he said my name with his German accent always caught my attention; it started like sarsaparilla and finished like a dance.

Niklas Wagner, star midfielder for the national soccer team the Santa Ana Saints, had come to me for a suit adjustment – yep by day I was the media officer for the Saints, and by night I designed; it was my hobby-cum-passion. Nik was standing in front of me wearing only the black suit pants and the jacket, no shirt – I could see all those well-developed abdominal muscles just waiting to be touched and I wouldn't mind tracing those grooves with my tongue either, up and down, tight and tense.

Is it getting hot in here? Then I accidentally did what I had been threatening, jabbed him with a pin.

'Ouch,' he yelped and stepped back.

'See? What did I tell you? Stand at attention,' I barked.

He stiffened and stood straight… for about five seconds.

'I like the gym gear you're wearing, Sah-sha, did you make that?' he asked looking down on my fitted black gym pants and matching tank top. It was easier to do fittings in fitted gym gear, easier to get around the fabric and the client, if that makes sense.

I shook my head. 'I don't make gym gear yet. But I am going to do a gym workout when you leave,' I said, with a glance to my home gym in the corner of the room.

'We should work out together,' he said.

I laughed. 'Stand still and stop looking down; it makes the pants longer.'

'What? Why is the idea of working out together funny?' he asked, frowning.

'It's funny because I would lift a thimble compared to you and you'd give me a hard time.'

'Never,' he said. 'I respect any workout; I'd love to see you in action Sah-sha. We could put some music on, work up a sweat, you know? Okay, I have to stop thinking about that now,' he said, and wiped a hand over his mouth.

Oh yes, he did indeed need to stop thinking about it. The bulge in his pants would change the line of them and the amount I had to take up.

'Should I readjust the measurements or assume when you wear these pants, you won't be, um, quite as stiff?' I asked looking up from the floor at him, trying to get a reaction.

He grinned. 'It depends. Will you be coming to the Best and Fairest Awards with me?'

'I'll definitely be there, working that night,' I said. 'So I'll leave the measurements as they are. Okay, you're done, get it off.'

He grinned again. I swear everything I said had a sexual connotation to this guy. He extended his hand like a gentleman and helped me off the floor. Phew, that was a rush, coming up past his bulge, then past the muscles in his bare chest and standing full height with my hand feeling so small in his. *I think I just orgasmed.* I looked away quickly.

'Thanks, you can let my hand go now,' I said, he did so slowly, running his fingers up my palm. *Holy fuck.*

I guess we had been flirting – if you could call it that – for a few weeks now and Nik was trying to get me to go out with him this weekend on our first official date. Tonight, however, the suit adjustment was business only. Maybe and it was a big maybe, on Friday night Niklas Wagner could take me out for dinner. Apart from deciding if I wanted to go out, I was considering whether to have sex with him before then and whether to order an entrée or save room for dessert. All tough decisions.

'C'mon Sarsh, aren't you going to help me take it off?' he said.

'So we're on nickname terms now?' I said, and narrowed my eyes at him. 'Sasha, Sash-a,' I said, rolling it off my tongue. 'C'mon, practice.'

'Sarsh like sarsey?' he said.

'Never mind,' I said. 'You know the way to the change room.'

He looked a little dejected as I pointed him towards the guest room which I had set up for clients. It included hanging racks, mirrors, a sofa and a small en-suite bathroom.

'Look even Prada thinks you should help me,' he said, with a glance at my black Bombay cat who had moved closer to us and now sat watching Nik warily.

I smiled at Prada, such a handsome puss. 'Trust me, he's not giving you that look because he is on your side,' I warned Nik, 'he's deciding whether to jump on your head or not. He's not very social.'

'Oh,' Nik said and moved a step farther away from where Prada was perched near the window. 'This is a great place. Is that your bedroom up there?' His eyes looked to my lofty room.

'Yes, that's where I sleep and entertain my lovers,' I teased him and he laughed. 'Now get changed.' Even though he towered over me, I tried giving him a direct order and pointed to the guest room. Call it girl power… maybe not, he was still standing there frowning at me. Man, this guy was persistent; he was trying every trick in the *How to Trap a Girl To Take Her on an Official Date* book. I studied him. He was the biggest potential 'boyfriend' on my scene for some time, maybe because I had removed myself from the scene some time ago. And when I say big, I'm not just talking height from the sneak preview I'd had – you can get very close to the anatomy when you're pinning a client.

It would be very easy to fall for Niklas Wagner. He looked as though he was still in the military with his short blond back and sides, but the top was long enough to run my hands through. My hair was almost the same color, only messier – since I had decided to grow it again I hadn't bothered cutting it, so it was a mess of long lengths. Nik's haircut, along with his tan, set off his bright blue eyes and even though he was fluent in English, his German accent still made for a direct manner of speech. We were suited there too – I was always in trouble for being too direct. That's where the similarities ended – I was five-foot-eight to his six-foot-plus, and I was pale to his tan.

'What if I accidentally get stabbed by a pin when I take it off?' he asked, his lips curling in a smile. 'It could penetrate an artery and put me out of play. The coach would be very upset with you Sah-sha.' He put his hands in the pockets of his suit pants and rocked back on his heels. Sexy as all fuck.

'Niklas.' I tried not to smile, which didn't work, while I crossed my arms across my chest. That only served to bring his eyes to my chest. 'You managed to put that suit on all by yourself, taking it off is pretty much the same only in reverse. You can do it; I have full faith in you. Should I do a Saints' war cry for motivation?'

He looked vaguely interested in the idea, but that look changed to a different expression – one that said he wasn't quite beaten yet. His jaw locked with frustration as he planned his next move – I suspect he was a man used to getting his own way with the women and trust me, since his arrival there was no shortage of women throwing themselves at him at the club and wherever the team socialized, from what I heard. I wouldn't know; being a groupie wasn't my thing.

He slipped the jacket off in front of me and strode off to the bedroom. I breathed out. I had won that round and enjoyed the spectacle of his muscles departing the room. Moments later he started up again.

'Sah-sha,' he called out from the guest room, 'I need your help.'

I shook my head. *Men. I'll give him help in a moment.* Ha, I sounded like my mother then.

'Coming,' I said. Yeah, he'd make something of that too I bet. *I'd love to come by the hand or tongue of Nik*; again with the sex thoughts. I really was too frustrated for my own good, but it was impossibly hard not to think about sex when you have a perfect specimen of manhood in your guest room.

I stalled him while I packed my sewing kit. I was just a little bit impressed that Nik wanted to get his suit adjusted because he had lost weight and didn't want to buy a new suit for a club award night. I liked the fact that he was on a contract worth more than this week's lottery draw, but he still wanted to get a suit adjusted rather than buy a new one, I hated waste too. When he mentioned he needed to find someone to do the adjustments, his housemate Alice – who happens to work with me at the Saints – told him I sew, wasn't that handy? Since they began flatting together, Alice had become the unofficial source of all Nik gossip, telling me all his movements even when I didn't want to know.

I had met Nik at the office of course before I played with his inside leg – a dressmaking term. You can't be media officer for the Santa Ana Saints soccer team and not know the players or at least talk to them by telephone to organize media interviews. He had only joined the club late last year, but we had spoken on the phone heaps of times when I was setting up pre-publicity for his arrival – *Germany's hottest recruit signed to the Saints*, the *Berlin wonder boy* or *'wunderkind'* if you translate it. Everyone wanted a piece of the 'Kaiser' and he was very obliging, doing all my telephone interview requests and there were heaps of them. His management team was really helpful with photos too, and as soon as he got off the plane, Shayne the Saints' football manager had Nik in the Saints' jersey and getting photos done before the poor guy even had time to unpack.

Nik cost the club a fortune, so I know he had a shitload of pressure on him to perform on-and-off the field for the club. Guys like Nik, the team's captain Lucas, goalkeeper Tomás and our forward The Russian had the pulling power to bring in memberships and ticket sales and to make the club big. Nik was definitely big. I wondered if he left someone behind in Berlin.

We finally met in the flesh for the first time when he came in to see Alice about a housemate position. He gave me an electric shock, way to make a first impression! Alice said it was an omen that we were suited and that we would always have a spark between us. Sounded like crap to me, but whatever, if it makes her happy to dream up this shit.

'Sah-sha? Are you coming in here?' Nik called again.

'Any minute now,' I answered, 'just cleaning up.'

'Can you make it quick?' he yelled back.

'Sure,' I said, slowing down. *Man must think I'm an idiot.*

Which reminded me of the next time I saw Nik in the flesh when I came off looking like the idiot… it was at a home game a few weekends back. Unfortunately, that didn't go well either. My job on game days is looking after the media and one of the journos from the daily paper wanted to talk with Nik before the game. Sometimes the coach allowed that. I chased down Shayne the football manager, who said Nik was getting iced and strapped so just go in and ask him. Unfortunately his groin was getting strapped when I walked in, so that's more evidence of how I know he's big all over. Yep, a fine import from Germany. Now on our third encounter, I'd stuck a pin in him, no wonder he was completely taken with me, what man could resist? Makes you wonder why he persisted; that guy must love a challenge.

'Sah-sha, seriously I need your help,' he called again, his voice a bit muffled this time. *What the fuck, has he got caught in his zip or something?* I smiled at his persistence, I love a man on a mission, and I headed to the guest room. Nik sat on the end of the sofa, the suit completely off and he was wearing a very nice pair of black fitted boxers. Blood poured from his nose and he cupped his face with one hand and used the other to keep himself upright on the bed. His tanned face had turned pale and his eyes were a little hazy.

'Holy fuck,' I said, and ran to the adjoining bathroom. Thank God my towels were navy in color. So not important right now but later, I'd be pleased. I ran back to his side, spread one across his lap covering his prize bounty and gave him one to hold against his nose.

'Sit up straight and tip your head forward,' I said, and

when he had done this, I pinched the soft part of his nose with my thumb and forefinger. I knew that the first aid course Aunty Sandra gave me for my birthday would come in handy – I love practical gifts.

'It's okay, I've got it,' he said with a muffled voice.

'Take over the pinch and I'll get an ice pack,' I said, removing my hand. I glanced into his eyes and they were not focusing on me.

'Think I should call Chris?' I asked him, referring to the team doctor.

'No,' he said, firmly, his eyes finding mine. They weren't clear, not good.

'Hmm.' I studied him.

'Really, no,' he said again. 'The ice pack would be good, thanks.' He sounded as though someone had punched him in the nose. I gave him a look that said I wasn't convinced but from what I knew of Nik already, he probably thought that look said I thought he was hot even when bleeding on my sofa. He kind of was actually, it was the boxer briefs and the muscles in his arms as he leaned forward… *right, get the ice.*

I raced into the kitchen, and decided to ignore Nik – I made a quick call to the team doctor. Talking quietly under my breath to Chris, I grabbed a tea towel and broke the ice cubes out of a tray from the freezer and into it. I balled it up, thanked the doc, hung up and took the ice back to the room. Nik was lying flat along the full length of the sofa now, his head propped at one end, and his legs overhanging at the other end. I could see all his muscles defined lying like that, including the main one in his boxer briefs.

'Nik, you need to sit for a while,' I said, kneeling in front of him.

'I need to lie, bit dizzy,' he mumbled. He held out his hand for the ice pack and I gave it to him and watched as he pressed it against his face.

'Doc should know about this,' I said, concerned, and with the quick reflexes Nik had developed from being a central midfielder, he grabbed my wrist, assuming I was going off to call when I was really justifying my actions.

'It's okay,' he said, and pulled me down beside him. 'Just stay next to me for a minute.'

I pulled away and grabbed the red cotton blanket from the end of the sofa – another excellent color choice for the occasion – and brought it up and over Nik to his waist given the ice was chilling him. I sat on the ground beside him, watching him. I instinctively rubbed his back – I'm very supportive of the ill – and scanned his face.

'How did this happen?' I asked.

He kept his eyes closed and shook his head slightly. 'Don't know, it just did. It'll be over in a minute.'

'Shh, just relax, you're not going anywhere,' I said. I'm sure he wanted to hear that earlier, not now when he was groggy and bleeding. I noticed some scars on his chest. I hadn't noticed them before, maybe because his tattoos run over some of them, but I could see now that they were small and he had quite a few. Strange. Not the best time to ask him about it while he was bleeding.

Ten minutes later, I heard the buzzer to my apartment and jumped up to let Chris in. The team takes all player injuries very seriously, especially when we're talking about the big contracted stars like Nik. I showed him through to the guest room. Nik groaned on seeing him, but the doctor said I was right to call.

'It's nothing,' Nik was muttering to the doctor. 'Sah-sha shouldn't have bothered you.'

'Let me be the judge of that. Sasha did the right thing,' Chris was saying. 'Look at me, Nik.'

I left them alone while I went to get Nik some water. He might be staying the night after all, in the guest room. I doubted he could climb the stairs to my loft in his current condition and I'm guessing he weighed more than I've ever pressed so I wouldn't be carrying him.

When I got back, the doc had righted him on the sofa and propped him up in sitting position, several of my decorated pillows behind him. The colors in the guest room really were working well for brides and nose bleeds; good to know I got that right. Nik was still a bit pale and he accepted the water and drank. Doc was taking his blood pressure. The next minute, there were two paramedics at the door and Nik was going out the door on a gurney. He was protesting but looked groggy.

'Should I call anyone?' I said, half to Nik and with a glance to the doc.

'No,' Nik answered quickly and tried to rise.

Doc pushed him back on the gurney. 'Nik, I'll meet you at the hospital. Just relax, you're not getting out of going,' he said, and gave the paramedics a nod.

'Thanks for calling me,' Doc said, turning to me.

'But what happened? Is it serious?' I asked, watching them wheel Nik out.

'His blood pressure is really low. That's probably why he's dizzy. I suspect it's nothing to worry about but they can observe him overnight just to be on the safe side and release him in the morning,' he said. 'Sorry to ruin the date.'

I shook my head. 'He came over to get a suit adjusted.'

Doc gave me a look that said he hadn't heard that one before.

'Why would he have low blood pressure?' I persisted.

The doc framed his answer. 'Athletes and people who exercise regularly tend to have lower blood pressure … but if he's dehydrated or not eating right, not getting enough vitamins, folate, got an infection, loss of blood… and it is a little warmer here than in Berlin, Nik's adapting his lifestyle.'

'Ah yeah, I get the picture thanks,' I said, glazing over. Clearly, Nik needed to eat more and drink more. I saw the doc out and went to clean up the room.

That was the third strange encounter now with Niklas Wagner. If I was him, and for the good of his career, I'd be keeping as far away from me as possible.

Chapter 2

I got to work around the usual time and walked into the Saints administration office which was at their playing grounds. It made it easier on game day if you forgot something, plus when the boys trained on the oval some afternoons it was great to check their progress too – uh huh, well that's what we girls tell ourselves while we check out their form. I carried a bag of Nik's clothes with me; I kept the suit to adjust it but I had his jeans, sneakers and sweatshirt to give to Alice to take home to him.

I walked past my boss's office and called out good morning. Jim, the Marketing Director, was great – mid-forties, wiry, funny, and as bosses go, I got lucky. I got around the corner to the partition area and stopped dead.

'What the…? Did I miss a meeting?' I looked from Alice to Kay. Alice beat me in half of the time but Kay never, ever beat me in. Kay was in her late thirties, a mom of two and a big lady – she looked after the club memberships.

'School holidays darling,' she said, with a grin. 'The hubby has a week off too. I swanned out of the house this morning as though I was in my early twenties and only had myself to worry about,' she said, teasing us both.

'Holy crap, not sure I'll recover from the shock,' I said, hitting my chest to restart my heart. I turned to face Alice. 'And why are you here early?' I glanced at Miss Fashion-plate. I loved my fashion designing but Alice just loved to shop. We were well placed opposite each other in the office. She even surprised me once by ordering one of my designs online under an alias and wearing it to a Saints' function. She was one of the good girls.

'I spent the night at Tomás's place,' she said of her Saint's player and Latin lover boyfriend, '… and he had training at six. So I've been up, done hot yoga, showered, changed and here I am. I've done a day's work already. I love your hat,' Alice said, 'truly suits you.'

'It's the Parisian influence today,' I said, patting it.

'Sasha always looks fabulous,' Kay said. 'I forget to notice. I'm so used to it.'

'Thanks you two, you're too kind.' I smiled and removed my small-brimmed cream-colored wool hat which just happened to match my belt and shoes. I love hats and gloves; I wish women still wore them every day, so I'm doing my bit to keep hats alive.

'Where's the coffee van?' Jim yelled from his office next door to us. It didn't require an answer, he yelled random things often during the day, and we had learned to ignore him.

I sighed and sank behind my desk, stretched down my navy and cream striped, ribbed top and spread out my short pleated navy skirt so I didn't crease it too much – so tricky sitting in pleats.

'Now Sasha, down to business… what did you do to my housemate last night?' Alice frowned. 'Nik still wasn't home when I left.' She gave me a sly look. 'Did you have a good night?'

I logged into my computer before looking over at her. I could feel Kay was waiting in suspended animation for my answer too.

Alice didn't know Nik had already asked me out to dinner on Friday night and she was still working at getting us together. I should put her out of her misery, but it was more fun playing her along.

'As obvious as your attempts are to set us up, Alice my dear,' I said in the most formal accent I could muster for the occasion, 'we did not have a lovely romantic night together. Even though for some, adjusting a tall, handsome, fit man's suit could count for foreplay, especially taking an inside leg measurement, that wasn't the case last night.' I held up a bag of clothes. 'Speaking of which can you give these back to Nik please?'

I saw Kay reach for a piece of paper to fan herself and Alice just looked bewildered.

'If he didn't stay the night and you have his clothes, where is he and is he naked?' Alice looked seriously worried now, as though I would kick Nik out on the street in nothing… imagine the stampede.

Before I could respond, we all stopped to pause as we heard the familiar loud footsteps of The Russian coming

en-route to his office next door to ours where the Saints'
forward ran his business – Security Saints. I'm pretty sure
The Russian's business partner and Saint's defender Eddie
Mosley did most of the work.

'Where's the coffee van?' The Russian asked, all six-foot-
five of him stomping past.

'Morning Russian,' Alice and Kay said in unison.

'Gee Russian, good to see you. I'll place a call and find
out where the hell she is since you're now in,' I said. I had
such a big mouth.

I saw his lips twitch into a smile or a smirk; it could go
either way really – The Russian was very hard to read.

'Morning ladies. By the way Sasha, I picked up Nik from
outpatients this morning after I brought some clothes up
for him to wear home. You need to be a bit gentler with
the Kaiser in future.' He strode off this time with a definite
sneaky smile on his face.

'What happened?' Alice asked.

'Thank God,' Jim yelled out and I guessed what that was
about. I turned to glance out the window as the coffee van
pulled in.

'Coming?' I asked Alice. I jumped up, and spent a few
minutes getting Kay and Jim's order to avoid the Spanish
inquisition – or in this instance the German inquisition – as
Alice followed me out of the office to the van to help with
the team's coffee hit. For the love of coffee, The Russian was
in front of me in the queue again. He gave me another smile.

'How did you get in front of me? You didn't even pass my
desk!' I wailed. Every single time he beat me to the van, and

it was infuriating. 'You suck, Russian,' I told him, which just made him laugh.

'I just happened to have walked around to see Shayne when it arrived, which is very close to the exit.' He gave me a satisfied look.

'I'll be verifying that story Russian,' I told him. Shayne the football manager and I worked closely together, so he'd spill. Alice and I suspected that The Russian got a pre-arrival text from the coffee lady herself. Somehow he'd charmed her into it – I'm a journalist, I'm not letting this go, I will investigate; I have my ways.

As we waited in line, we heard the familiar sound of a motorbike and Alice's face lit up as Tomás arrived on his black Ducati, looking divine in leather. This job was so hard – so hard to concentrate on the real work at hand – which reminded me I had a couple of press releases to write this morning and I had to wash down some media speculation about Niklas arriving in an ambulance to emergency last night. Damn him for making work for me.

Tomás parked his bike, turned it off and walked towards us, saying hello to The Russian at the start of the queue until he got six places down farther to us.

'Al...iss, long time no see,' he teased her, his hand going to her shoulder. He wasn't allowed to kiss her at work – Alice was new and she was keen on keeping up professional standards. I'd been there a while now so whatever, they knew me.

Tomás noticed me next. 'Hello, Sass...sha.'

'Morning Tomás,' I said, smiling at his lovely sexy

pronunciation of my name in his Spanish tongue. We moved one place forward again in the coffee queue.

'I heard you put the Kaiser in hospital last night,' he said, and made a tsk sound with that very same tongue. 'You'll have to go softer on him from now on, he's not as tough as me or The Russian,' he said, as The Russian walked down the line towards us with coffee in hand.

'What happened?' Alice asked again, turning her attention to me.

Tomás grinned. 'Got to see Shayne. I'll catch you on the way out, Bella,' he said to Alice and walked into the building with The Russian.

I shook my head. And just to make my day, guess who pulled into our parking lot next in his navy blue VW sports utility with his surfboard strapped to the roof racks? Yep, the sickie himself, Nik. Just kill me now… I glanced to the office to gauge whether I could get back in there before he alighted. No such luck. He got out of his vehicle and I had to hand it to him, he looked good, really good. He must have gone straight from the hospital home to change and to the beach – he had red-print board shorts on, a gray loose long-sleeve T-shirt and white sneakers. His short hair looked ruffled where it had enough length to hold the sand and sea. He looked good enough to lick. He greeted the remaining five office staff in front of us ordering coffee and stopped in front of Alice and me.

Alice looked up at him, squinting her eyes. 'I just heard you were in hospital last night. I thought you were sleeping over at Sasha's… are you okay?'

'I'm fine; it was nothing.' He smiled at her and then turned to me. 'Hello Sah-sha, sorry about last night. I promise to do better next time.'

I grimaced, knowing the remaining office staff in the line would all think we were on.

'It wasn't a date, so no big deal,' I said, with a shrug. 'But yeah, most guys don't bleed for me.'

'I like to go that extra mile,' he said. His tongue licked his lower lip and it was all I could do to not knock him to the ground and suck it. Alice nudged me back to reality, as the queue moved up closer to the prize coffee machine.

'Nik, if I were you, I'd get right away from me… we're about to enter the boiling milk zone.'

He shuddered, held up his hands and stepped back.

'I've got to catch up with Doc, but I'm telling you Sah-sha, we're not jinxed,' he said. 'Friday?'

'Mm,' I said. 'Maybe.'

'Come on, really?' He extended his hands in front of him. Then he must have remembered where we were and that we weren't alone.

'We'll talk,' he said with a departing look. It sounded more like an order than a request.

I saluted and clicked my heels together.

Nik glanced back. 'I saw that.' He waved a finger at me as he entered our reception area.

Alice laughed beside me and then hit my arm. 'You didn't tell me you had a date with Nik?'

'Didn't I?' I frowned. 'Mm, must have slipped my mind. Besides, I haven't said yes to the date yet, I'm thinking about it.'

'You're a strange one Sasha,' she said, narrowing her eyes at me.

Brenda, the CEO's personal assistant who was ahead of me in the queue, had turned to watch Nik enter the building. She touched my arm. 'Wild beasts would have to keep me from a date with Niklas, oh my he's something,' she said.

'We haven't had wild beasts attack yet, but don't tempt fate, Brenda,' I warned her and she laughed.

'Can you make mine a double shot please?' I asked Wendy, our coffee van lady, as I finally arrived at the top of the queue. I gave her Kay and Jim's order too. Then I went back to thinking about Nik. It's a good thing he is gorgeous, or I'd make that suit so tight in all the wrong places he'd never sit comfortably. I smiled at the wicked thought; good grief, what was wrong with me?

*****

Back at my desk, I drummed up a statement that diffused any rumors about Nik being taken to the hospital overnight – a flat comment from the football manager just to shut it down. Then I whipped up a press release promoting this Sunday's game which included information on the Saints, our current injury list, the Chicago Cats that we were playing against, how many times we'd won and lost against them in the last five years and other bits and pieces. I would send it out today to get interviews and interest for the week kicked off, and then send an updated version again on Friday with the current team list for the weekend.

I swanned around to see Shayne who signs off on my press releases and he had Nik, Tomás, and young striker Harry in his office. Lucky bastard. I waved the paper at him and told him I would come back. I could feel the eyes of all three men observing me, especially Nik who had an expression on his face as though he knew me better today having been in my apartment... maybe he did.

'Hey Sash, all good, leave them with me and I'll get them back to you in thirty minutes,' Shayne said. Ah, Shayne, so lovely – a former player who was still great eye candy and so sweet. I smiled and thanked him, pushing my way through the wall of muscle men in his office. I could barely squeeze in or squeeze out. The workplace hazards I had to put up with; it was disgraceful. Inching my way out, I returned to my side of the building and flagged with Jim that I was whipping over to do a quick stocktake of merchandise. We might need some new stock before the weekend's game – well that was my story, I really just needed to breathe some air that Nik wasn't sucking in at the same time. Plus, I didn't want a date debate in the office. This way, I would be out of the office if Nik did a loop past looking for me. I'm brilliant the way I come up with solutions sometimes.

As I did my stock take, I thought about Niklas Wagner – he was like a dog with a bone. I wasn't convinced he really was that interested me. Hell, he could have his choice of women. I think he couldn't understand why I wasn't falling at his feet so he had to keep gnawing away at me. If he could conquer me, so to speak, he'd probably lose interest. *Good luck buddy because I'm onto you and frankly, I'm busy.*

I didn't want to go out with a player and I needed another bossy boyfriend like I need another pair of black high heels – you know how it is, certain heel lengths suit some outfits better, hell I must have at least eight pairs. Is that too many? I must ask Alice.

I was doing just fine at the moment, enjoying my space, loving my Saints' work, having time to design and sew after hours and feeling good about myself. I didn't have time for a guy. Yep, I was just where I wanted to be – feeling on top, in charge, focused, and happy.

I just had to get Nik out of my head since he'd somehow managed to work his way in there. Damn that hot body, sexy smile, crystal blue eyes and big… well, features! Yep, I'm doing a great job of not thinking about him.

Chapter 3

I walked into my apartment, closed the door and breathed out. Coming home was my favorite part of the day – my pad was on the top floor of a four-story block and I guess it was more like an attic with four large triangle-shaped windows running from the floor to ceiling and looking skyward. It was my escape, my hideaway; I got it for a bargain given Dad was in property development and when I bought it, it was just a big open plan room. I've designed it with a catwalk right down the middle of the room, made of timber and about two feet off the ground. My brother Jason made it for me. When I'm doing fittings, most of the girls love it when I get them to do a run of the catwalk to see how their outfit falls as they walk. For the brides, it's like walking down the aisle. Some nights I put on the music and just dance along with it for a workout, and it's been a while since gymnastics but I can do four front flips in quick succession allowing enough room so I don't fall off the end.

I also have a platform for brides and girls getting formal dresses to stand on when I'm fitting. It is a perfect timber square and about a foot off the ground. It shows the fall of the dress and with all the fabric and often petticoats of tulle, it lets me check every layer is where it should be. One wall is also all mirrors for clients to see their outfits and for me when I'm doing my gym workout. I push myself harder if I can see the muscles working. The mirrors also reflect the trees outside and as luck would have it, I had a great view of Nik's back, shoulders and butt reflected in the mirror while I was fitting his front. Yep, when it comes to room design, I'm not just a pretty face!

Along the windows, I have three antique mannequins that look super cool, a row of vintage hat boxes and hat stands, and two small two-seater white leather sofas facing each other but separated by a glass coffee table. A big screen television hangs on the wall and that's my living area.

My bedroom's on a timber suspended floor that juts out from the wall, supported by poles and reachable by a spiral staircase. There was no way Nik was going to get up there in his state last night. Underneath it was my private bathroom with a big bath and frosted glass shower doors that led to some great shadows if you wanted a peek show. On the other side of the room was the guest room and en-suite with the Nik-christened-sofa – he was the first Saints' player ever to lie there and, I hoped, the last. Plus, I had a special cat run near the large triangle windows for Prada. He loves to look outside and watch the birds in the branches of the trees and on the eaves. Mom's worried that at twenty-three I'm too young to live alone, but I love my space and my place. I'm surrounded by people all day and here I can just let my imagination wander, play my music and create.

I gave Prada a hug, asked him about his day as I prepared his dinner and then changed into some jeans and a black hoodie. I heard my phone ping with a text. That would be Saffron my sister – twin sister – late as usual. She was coming over to discuss her wedding dress for the big day in ten months' time – a big church wedding with one hundred and thirty guests, so far – and she was trusting me to make her dress. We were going to buy the four bridesmaids' dresses, thank fuck for that, and of course the theme color was purple, the color of the saffron flower.

I was kind of envious, not of Saffron or of her getting married, nope all good with that, but she was marrying a guy whose surname was Flowers. So envious – she'll go through life now as Saffron Flowers... I wish. My sister was a primary school teacher – she loved children and so did her fiancé who was also a teacher. They intended to have hundreds of kids which I was very pleased about – if they could just replace themselves and me in the world, that would take a lot of pressure off me.

I grabbed my phone but the message wasn't from Saffy, it was from Nik. I glanced to the clock; he must have just finished training.

NIK: So, Sasha, are we on for Friday? Would love to show you a good time!

Big head! Prada brushed against me and then leaped to his favorite position near the window where he could look down on the world.

'I know he's gorgeous,' I told Prada, as I paced the

room, 'and I'd love to see him naked but this is not going to go anywhere good.' I looked to Prada again and he was listening attentively – he's a great listener. I continued to tell Prada about Nik. 'He's a player, on-and-off the field, Puss, most of the team is like that, that's the life they lead. He has a two-year contract and then he might go home to Berlin or somewhere.'

Me, well I didn't tell Prada, but eventually I want to travel the world too. Absorb inspiration and design, write about the experience, live for months on end in Paris, London, New York, Melbourne, Amsterdam… Nik, well he's a speed bump. I drew a deep breath and typed a message.

ME: Hey Nik, going to pull the pin, dressmaking speak. But thanks.

There was a knock at the door, and I sent the message, dropped the phone back on the kitchen island and went to let Saffy in.

'Sash,' she squealed two decibels higher than the average ear can bear and embraced me in an all-encompassing hug. 'I've got it – the fabric and the perfect pattern.'

'I never doubted that for a minute,' I teased her.

She rushed in and I closed the door behind her. Her long brunette hair was tied up in a ponytail, and she wore fitted gym wear. We couldn't be more different: Saffron was full-figured, I was a stick; Saffy was a few inches shorter than me and she was tanned while I was lean and as white as milk, usually – Saffy had been trying spray tans for her wedding which means I was trying spray tans with her… does kind of make you wonder what I'm doing living near the beach.

'Hello Prada, you handsome puss,' she greeted my black cat as he leaped down and came over to welcome her. I watched Saffron patting him; she caught me staring and smiled.

'Are you okay, Sash?' she asked.

'I'm great. Coffee, drink, are you hungry?'

'No thanks, I've got to be at Daniel's place in an hour. We're looking at invitations tonight, so exciting. But you go ahead,' she said, with just a hint of hope that I didn't.

'Nope, let's get right to it,' I said, and watched her brighten.

'I love your place,' she looked around. 'We're going to move into Daniel's apartment when we get married, but we're saving for something with a yard. Dad's on the lookout for us.'

'You'll need a yard for all those kids,' I said, and rolled my eyes.

Saffron saw my expression and laughed. 'You'll love being Aunty Sasha, I know it.'

'You know more than me,' I told her. 'Hand it over.'

She reached into the shopping bag she was carrying and pulled out the pattern.

'Ta-da!' she announced and I looked at her and smiled before I looked at the pattern. I slowly looked down and she laughed.

'Oh Saff, it's gorgeous.' I breathed a sigh of relief. I knew she was a traditionalist but this was perfect and would suit her – an elegant sweetheart neckline and an A-line dress with a flared skirt. 'It's you; you'll look breathtaking.'

I looked up as she blinked tears from her eyes and I squeezed her hand.

'Right, let's check your measurements.' I took a new set of her measurements and took a peek at the beautiful fabric she had selected. 'Perfect.' I put it back in the bag. 'Okay, Friday night I'm cutting,' I warned her.

'You're not going out?' she asked.

'What? No, Prada and I are staying in, two pussies in the house! So if you change your mind about the pattern and the fabric, you have until then, right? Because after that, snip, snip,' I said, and imitated the scissors cutting.

'Right,' she agreed. She grabbed her purse to depart and gave me a kiss on the cheek. I walked her to the door.

'Say hi to Daniel for me,' I told her. 'Tell him I'm happy to do his mom's dress and thanks for asking.' I opened the door and nearly got tapped on my forehead – raising his hand to knock was Nik. He looked from Saffron to me and back.

'Hi Sah-sha,' he started. He looked hot, unbelievably hot, but he didn't look happy at all. His brow was furrowed and his eyes were glaring at me with a look that said please explain.

'Nik! What are you doing here?' I asked, swallowing. I knew exactly what he was doing here. He wasn't happy at my date turndown by message.

'Hello.' Saffron brightened and turned to me with a raised eyebrow. 'You sure you're cutting Friday night?'

'Um Niklas this is Saffron, Saffy meet Nik,' I introduced them.

'Hi Nik, good to meet you. Got to run,' Saffron said, and with that, she was out in the hallway. I saw her look back to admire him and she gave me a thumbs up. Then she was gone and I was alone with Nik, again. I looked down the hallway but couldn't follow her, bummer; there was no escape.

Chapter 4

We stood at the door staring at each other. I didn't want to invite him in because I had a fair idea where that would lead. I tried really hard not to admire how good he looked in the team track pants, a fitted long-sleeved T-shirt, and his sneakers… hot as hell. His hair was still damp from the club's showers, his arms were defined and his body tapered to lean hips and… focus.

'Did you get my message?' I asked him.

'Yes, Sah-sha, that's why I'm here. I don't understand it.' He met my eyes with a cool blue gaze and blinked, waiting to be enlightened.

'But, it was simple English, oh hang on, pull the pin, didn't make sense, sorry.'

'I understood the term.' His eyes flashed. 'I don't understand why.' His voice had turned to ice, which instead of chilling me, made me super cranky. Why the hell did I have to explain anything to him?

'So, you can't take no for an answer?' I frowned at him.

'Apparently not.' He cleared his throat. 'If you are saying

no to the date because you think we're jinxed, then I'm going to prove that's not true,' he said. 'But, if you are saying no to the date because you can't see how manly, handsome and adorable I am Sah-sha, well we have a problem.' He had just the hint of a smile as he crossed his arms and leaned against the door frame.

I tried not to smile but it didn't work. I stood aside and he came in. He pulled his phone, wallet and keys from different pockets and put them down on my entrance table. I stayed near the kitchen open plan island and watched as he wandered around the room, glanced up to my bedroom loft and traced the stairs from the top down until he landed his gaze back on me. I could smell his freshness – soap, shampoo, deodorant, cologne, so manly. His presence in the house was distracting.

'Was that one of your friends or a client?' Nik asked after my sister.

'Why? Want to ask her out?' I asked.

The man just shook his head. 'No, Sah-sha, I want to ask you out, but I'm not having much luck.' He continued his tour of my place which he didn't cover in as much depth last night and looked out the windows.

'She's my twin sister,' I said.

Nik spun around to look at me. His hand went to his heart. 'No, there's two of you?'

I gave him a wry look. 'Yes, but we're very different, not identical.'

'I got that,' he said, and lowered himself to sit on the windowsill stretching one long leg out in front of him. He added a nice touch to that corner, and I wondered if I could talk him into staying there. I moved to lean on a stool in the living room where I could keep him in sight, just in case.

'There's actually five of us,' I said, 'I have three brothers as well… triplets.'

'Fuck, really? Are your parents rabbits?' Nik asked with a serious face. I grinned at the thought.

'Yes, they are, Mr. and Mrs. Bunny.' I rolled my eyes at him and he gave me a winning smile. That man belonged on the catwalk, preferably my catwalk.

'Mom and Dad couldn't have kids so they did IVF,' I explained. 'When Mom got pregnant she found out she was having triplets. She says it was a wonderful blessing – you can decide if you ever meet my brothers,' I said.

'I'm bound to meet them at all the family dinners we'll be having, Sah-sha,' he teased me. 'So how did you and your twin come on the scene?'

'Mom and Dad decided they wanted to try for a girl. They did another few cycles of IVF and then presto, but only two this time.'

'So Sarf-fron and Sah-sha. Is there an 's' theme happening with your big brothers?' he asked.

'Nope, nothing like that – Jason, Ethan and Sam. Jason is a carpenter. He built my catwalk and bridal stage; Ethan is a counselor; and, Sam is a mechanic.'

'Ah, so that's how you can afford to have an Alpha Spider… they are usually in the garage getting fixed.' Nik shook his head.

'Yes, how did you know I had a Spider?'

'I saw you leaving work when I was training. It suits you.'

'Mm, thanks. She's gorgeous, a series three. I wanted one for a long time and Sam kept an eye out, eventually finding one for me that I could afford. I pay him in kind – I dress him, he services the car.'

'No other men in your life?' he asked.

'Well, Mr. Direct, there's my best friend Max, and his partner Ren.'

'Ren is male or female?' Nik asked.

'Male. You got a problem with that?' I narrowed my eyes.

'What? With you having a best friend or him being gay? Why would I care?' Nik shrugged.

Good answer. I might have been a bit defensive then. We sat in silence for a few moments. God, even indifference looked sexy on him. Nik eventually broke it.

'I love your place, it's very cool and…' he looked at the catwalk, '… interesting. Do you model?'

I laughed but he said it in all seriousness.

'Uh no, it's for my clients and my workout,' I said.

'Yeah.' He grinned. 'How? Do you run up and down it?'

'No I dance on it or I do my handstands and flips.' I wish I hadn't said that because I knew straight away what was coming

'Great!' His face lit up. 'Show me Sah-sha.'

'I'm not dressed for it,' I said, looking down at my jeans, sneakers and hoodie.

'I'll spot you, come on,' he said, humor in his voice as though he didn't expect me to do it. Therefore, I had to do it.

'Fine, but I need to warm up,' I said. I stood up and removed my hoodie, revealing a light gray fitted cotton T-shirt underneath overhanging my jeans. Unfortunately the T-shirt read 'Journalists do it on the front', but hey, I wasn't expecting to be flashing it to Nik.

Nik laughed reading it. 'Can I help?' he asked, seductively. I've not doubt he could help me get to orgasm in under a minute but when it came to flips, I had them covered.

'I'm good,' I said. I walked to the catwalk and tucking just the front of my T-shirt into my hip-cut jeans so I didn't flash too much, I did a handstand, followed by a walk over front and back to warm up. Then I started down the end where Nik was sitting, took a deep breath and flipped down my catwalk, counting four and stopping with a final leap, back down and feet together.

Nik burst out in applause. 'Fantastic. Do it again,' he said.

'No, your turn,' I said, eyes narrowing on him. 'Show us your tricks.'

Nik grinned and stood up. 'I can't do that,' he said. 'I could probably pull off a handstand or two.' He reached for my hoodie and brought it over to where I stood on the catwalk. He held it out so I could slide my arms in, then he trapped me. He flipped me around pulling the front tightly around me, my face was level with his as I stood on the catwalk. He looked directly into my eyes, then to my lips and back to my eyes again. My breathing hitched.

'Why won't you go out with me, Sah-sha?' he asked in soft voice. 'Is there someone else?'

'No. Is there someone else in your life, or lots of someone elses?' I returned the question.

His eyes narrowed. 'Of course not. Why would I ask you out if there was someone else?' He continued to stare at me, keeping me pressed right against him at eye level.

'I'm not ready; I'm liking the space I'm in and...' My voice trailed off.

He didn't look convinced, not one bit.

'You've been hurt,' he said, directly. I spluttered trying to come up with some form of denial and he released me from his grip. 'We can take this very slowly, Sah-sha, I have all the time in the world,' he said.

His words calmed me and freaked me out in equal measure. All the time he watched me saying nothing.

'Everyone's been hurt,' I finally managed to get out, 'I'm just having time out to focus on work and my designing.'

'Right,' he said, again not looking at all convinced. 'Are you going to offer me a drink because I'd love a coffee, white with none.'

'Nik, would you like a coffee?' I asked.

'Thanks Sah-sha, that would be great,' he said, with a smile. He picked me up at the hips and lifted me down from the catwalk. So sexy, for fuck's sake.

I cleared my throat. 'Have you eaten?' I asked, knowing he wouldn't have since he probably came straight over from training.

'No, I'm fading away, but I'll last until you send me home.'

'Hell no. You got a nose bleed on me last time. I'm not calling Doc to say this time you've collapsed from lack of carbohydrates.' I waved a menu at him. 'There's a really good noodle place around the corner that delivers; what do you think?'

He grinned. 'You want me to stay? That's sweet Sah-sha. I trust you to order.'

I gave him a look that said *don't make a habit of this buddy.* He probably misread it to mean *I can't wait to feed you noodles* – we weren't really good with the comprehension. I flicked the kettle on and dialed the noodle bar whose number was in my phone.

'Anything you don't eat?' I asked.

'I'll taste anything,' he said, rising to join me in the kitchen. Again with the sexual reference, and now all I could think about was his tongue. When I pulled my gaze away from his mouth, I pointed to the cupboard and he found two coffee mugs. I waited on hold and directed him to a Lady Grey teabag for me and the coffee for him. I wondered if he knew that what he was saying was suggestive… the noodle bar answered their telephone.

'Hi Yuki, yeah it's me. Yes the usual please plus I've got a friend here so can I also get the teriyaki chicken with thick egg noodles, and the Mongolian beef with the same and a serve of steamed dim sims and the dumplings, plus two house salads with low-fat dressing, thanks. Yeah… he's very hungry. No, he's not fat, yet. Thanks, Yuki.' I hung up.

'You've got a friend here, huh?' Nik pulled the teabag out. 'You hurt me Sah-sha.'

'Boo hoo, you,' I said, and thanking him took my tea.

He stood about an inch from me. 'Sah-sha.' He said my name followed by a noise of sheer exasperation. I thought he was about to put me over his knee next and smack me for being naughty. He took a deep breath, getting his frustration under control, finished stirring milk in his coffee and moved back to the window. I joined him, taking the sofa while he took the windowsill. Prada watched, perched above.

'Now you know my family structure, tell me about yours,' I prodded.

I hit a nerve; Nik stiffened and I saw walls shutting down all around him. I could almost hear them clanking and locking in place.

'Nothing to tell, Sah-sha, no brothers or sisters. Speaking of which, you're clearly not identical to your twin sister,' he said. Interesting segue. I wondered what the story was there. He wouldn't get away with that though; research is my middle name. Actually, it's Elizabeth, but you get my drift.

I thought about my sister and me, and how we were anything but identical. 'No, my sister is like that *Carpenters* song, you know where the angels get together to make a dream come true?'

'No,' he said, flatly.

'Right, well just follow along,' I suggested. 'So the angels rock up and they decide to make this beautiful soul, who is pretty, gentle and affectionate. They sprinkled moon dust in her hair or something similar… whatever… anyway when they finish they put her in the womb to be born. But while they were doing that, one of them said 'hold up, crap, there's two eggs here.' Following me so far?'

Nik smiled and nodded. 'Is that part about the two eggs in the song?'

'No, from now on the rest of the story is all mine.'

'Go on,' he encouraged me.

'So these angels thought since they had perfection going on with the first one, they'd have to fish around for leftovers. Then one of them says, 'ah, I've got this changeling'… you know the folklore…'

'I know about changelings,' Nik said, listening attentively as though he enjoyed fairytales.

'So they agree, that's a perfect solution – they drop this skinny, blonde, white, reclusive changeling in next to perfection and the changeling falls madly in love with the perfect offspring and they live happily ever after,' I said, and sipped my tea.

Nik studied me, not smiling, not speaking. He sipped his coffee.

'Your sister seems very lovely, but you Sah-sha, you're…'

The doorbell rang and I rose quickly, trying not to spill my tea. 'That will be the noodles.'

'I've got this,' Nik said, putting his coffee down and with his long legs he got to the door before me, grabbing his wallet off the table on the way. He greeted the small Asian delivery guy who had to look up a foot or more to see him. Nik whipped out some notes to cover it and thanked the driver with a good tip.

'I'll give you half,' I said, pulling the dollars from my purse.

'No you won't,' he said. 'Plates?'

I gave him a frustrated look.

'I've got this Sah-sha, I'll eat most of it anyway,' he said.

'Okay, thanks, but you're wrong there,' I said, and put my cash away. I entered the kitchen to get us some plates and cutlery. 'I think you've mistaken me for one of the beautiful people who hang around you nibbling while they watch you eat, or purge up their food later. I'm not starving to watch my figure… I eat.'

'Great,' he said. 'We can try some different places. I haven't been anywhere good to eat since I got here and fuck, I'm hanging for a good meal. I'd really love to try some real restaurants.'

'Really? Is that why you've lost weight?' I looked at him surprised; I wouldn't have taken him for a food connoisseur.

He filled two glasses with water and shrugged. 'Lucas and I used to hang out a bit before he got a girlfriend, but he just got everything delivered. The Russian's single now, but he only eats meat…'

I laughed. 'Yeah that sounds like The Russian, you've got to keep moving around him or he's sizing you up as a meal,' I agreed.

Nik smiled and continued. 'If it is not spicy, Tomás won't eat it. Andy, do you know the PT?' he stopped to ask me.

I nodded. 'Sure, but not that well.'

'He and his wife have invited me around a few times for dinner,' he clarified. 'She can cook; he's lucky. So did Elizabeth, the coach's wife, but that's not the most comfortable meal… a thousand questions.'

I studied Nik as he gave an insight into what his first few months here had been like. I forgot he was probably a bit lonely, but at least now he was living with Alice and her friend, Cassie.

'That wouldn't be fun,' I agreed, reluctantly.

Nik brightened. 'I know, so go out with me?' He looked at me and gave me a smile that would melt any red-blooded girl.

We spread the dishes on the counter and helped ourselves. Nik tried some of my regular dishes and I tried the ones I ordered for him. It was weirdly comfortable, as though we were housemates who would soon be fighting over the remote.

'How do you feel about the remote?' I asked, just out of curiosity.

'I have to have it.'

'Hmm,' I said. 'Me too, especially in my house,' I added.

His eyes narrowed as he took that in.

'Buying dinner tonight is not replacing Friday night dinner when you dress up, I pick you up and take you somewhere nice. Right?' he asked.

I delayed my response while we moved to the sofa again and he joined me this time, abandoning the window sill. We sat on opposite sides to each other.

'Is this something you do… if a girl turns you down on a date you pursue her until she changes her mind?' I asked. 'Or do you just persist until you understand why you're not date material to every woman on the planet?' I wound some delicious noodles around my fork, taking a huge mouthful with no thought of being glamorous.

He shrugged. 'I've never been turned down before.'

I nearly choked on my noodles, finishing with a charming snort of derision.

'What?' I said, swallowing. 'How old are you?'

'Twenty-three,' he said. 'And you?'

'The same, twenty-three.'

'See we like our food and we're the same age, so many

things in common,' Nik teased, and I snorted again in a ladylike manner. I could understand why he was completely taken by me.

I continued my research. 'So let me clarify this… you've never been turned down before? You've asked women out though, right?'

Nik rolled his eyes. 'What do you think?'

'And you'd have a lot of women who hang around you and want to go out with you right?' I continued.

He shrugged. 'Yes, but you're the only woman I've asked out who doesn't find me attractive and won't go on a date with me.'

'I didn't say that… I mean clearly you're okay in the looks department,' I said. That shouldn't make his head too big.

'Thanks, wow, big compliment.' He feigned being overwhelmed. 'Hold on, any minute we both won't fit in here as my head expands,' he joked.

I grinned. 'Okay, you're good looking, happy now?'

'Very,' he said. 'About what you were saying before Sahsha, your sister is lovely, but you are gorgeous. I can't believe you can't see it,' he said.

I stopped, my fork suspended in mid-air and I looked at him. It wasn't fair saying stuff like that without any warning. I stuffed the noodles in my mouth and pretended I didn't hear it; I avoided looking at him but in my peripheral vision I could see him cock his head on the side and study me.

We sat in an awkward silence or maybe it was just me that felt awkward. I swallowed. 'Water top up?' I asked.

'Please,' he said. He put his unfinished meal down on the

coffee table and waited for me to return before eating. Nice. We ate our way through the meal. It was going well. Maybe we weren't jinxed after all, and as soon as I thought that, it happened again.

My husband arrived.

Chapter 5

I heard the knock on the door and looked at Nik. I'm very particular about my guests and I wasn't expecting a client.

'Are you expecting anyone?' I asked and he laughed.

'Yeah I gave out your address to everyone, told them to find me here,' he said, and continued eating.

I rose and went to the door. I barely had it opened a foot before my husband, photographer-cum-druggy Adam Lattimore stomped in. Just a bit taller than me, thin, hippy, artist, boy-next-door charm – he looked more like a musician in a band than a photographer.

'It's official, we're unofficial, babe, miss me yet?' he asked, and threw some paperwork on the kitchen counter.

Make that my ex-husband.

'Yeah, well thanks for bringing around the paperwork and see ya,' I said, still standing with the door open.

'Thought you might want to celebrate,' he smiled, grabbing my hips and pulling me close to him. He had a smile that was like a drug to me... insidious, dangerous, and tempting. He rocked a pair of jeans and a black long sleeve T-shirt, his dark brown hair was shaggy and flopped into his blue eyes and everything about him spelled danger to me. He was a shit husband. Then he spotted Nik.

'Who's this?' he asked, staring at Nik from the kitchen.

I heard Nik sigh before he rose, as if dealing with dickheads was part of the norm when dating a girl. He came towards us.

'This is a colleague of mine,' I said.

'A colleague?' Adam mocked me. Nik looked equally unimpressed. Adam was always insanely jealous; happy to play the field himself but woe betide me if I glanced at anyone.

'I'm the media officer for the Saints', Adam, and Nik is a Saint, so to speak,' I said, moving to stand between the two men. Nik was easily a foot or so taller and wider, but Adam was street smart.

I introduced them. 'Nik Wagner, Adam Lattimore.' Nik went to extend his hand to shake and Adam folded his arms. I felt Nik bristle beside me.

'Like them pretty now, do you?' Adam asked me.

'Actually I.Qs are in now, buddy,' Nik shot back and I laughed instinctively which was the wrong thing to do. Adam pushed me away to reach Nik and I hit the wall, he swung one good shot at Nik connecting with his eye and as Nik reeled back with the surprise hit, Adam took off. He was gone in seconds.

'Fucking hell.' Nik straightened and reached for me. 'Are you okay, Sah-sha?'

'I'm fine.' I straightened my clothes.

'Little punk.' Nik started out the door but I grabbed his arm, my hand barely going around half of the muscles in his arms.

'Nik, leave it, please,' I begged, 'please.'

Nik turned back to look at me, his jaw locked in frustration, but he walked back inside, closing the door. I hated to think what damage they might do to each other.

I touched his face and he flinched slightly. He was darkening slightly around one eye and he had a trickle of blood on his cheek from a cut. Adam's ring must have cut his face.

'I'm really sorry, Nik,' I said, studying his face. 'I know he doesn't deserve to get away with that.'

'It's okay, don't worry about it.' He shrugged.

'I will worry about it, now lean against the island,' I ordered him. He did what he was told which was refreshing. I opened a drawer in the kitchen where I had some basic first aid stuff and found some antiseptic.

'Stay put for a sec,' I said, and raced to the bathroom to grab tissues and cotton balls. I returned, dampened the cotton balls in warm water and cleaned the cut. His blue eyes watched me with just a hint of amusement and a bit of lust, well I think it was lust since we'd eaten already. I leaned up on my toes and touched some antiseptic against the cut.

'Ouch, Sah-sha.' He pulled away from me.

'Don't be such a baby,' I said, returning to pat his face. He closed his eyes and let me. He really was gorgeous; I could just kiss those lips while he leaned there looking so peaceful. 'There, that's done. You won't be as pretty for a while, but some girls like rugged.'

'That so?' he asked with interest.

'So I've heard. I'll make you another coffee while you sit and hold some ice to your eye. Go relax,' I said.

'Hmm.' He grunted and headed back to the sofa. He began to clean up our plates on the coffee table and I ordered him to leave it. It was good that he followed orders so easily. I must remember that, could come in handy at work too.

I came over with a tea towel laden with ice cubes – déjà vu from his last visit – and handed them to him. Instead of taking the ice, he took my hips.

'You put it on,' he said, and pulled me closer. I guess it was the least I could do and he did look like he needed some tender lovin' care. I bit my lip and hesitated just a moment knowing where this might lead. He took the decision away from me, and pulled me down onto his lap to straddle him, all the time he kept his hands around my hips. He leaned his head back on the sofa seat and closed his eyes. I applied the ice to his bruised socket and he winced slightly at the sting of cold.

'I'm really sorry, Nik,' I whispered. 'I told you we were jinxed.'

'We're not jinxed, Sah-sha,' he growled. 'You've just got a dickhead…'

'Ex-husband,' I said, finishing for him. It was the first time I had said ex-husband out loud and I felt a tinge of pain. I had loved Adam once, maybe still loved the Adam I remembered. Now it was officially over. I was a divorcee at twenty-three – my first real-life failure.

'How long were you married?' he asked.

'Four years. We met when I was studying journalism; I was nineteen, he was twenty-four. He's a photographer, works for *The Daily*. We met on a job – there was this artist getting great reviews for his avant-garde work. So, the college magazine sent me to cover it and he was there for the paper. I guess we just clicked. We were married three months later – my folks hated him.'

'Yeah, well I can imagine them not being too excited,' Nik said. 'They have this clever girl at college with a bright future and she runs off and marries a photographer she's known for a minute who is older and more advanced than she is.'

'Yeah, thanks Dad for summing that up,' I said. Nothing I hadn't heard before.

Nik chuckled and repositioned himself slightly under me – great we could both feel it now, his huge erection pressing through his training pants against my jeans. Apologies if I'm *squashing* it.

'It's not like I gave up college or anything just because we got hitched,' I told him, 'but it was a pretty wild ride. Anyway Saffron's the reliable one, I'm sure they expected nothing less from me.' I continued to defend myself which is strange because I never really gave a fuck what people thought and probably still don't. Why did I need to make myself look better in Nik's eyes?

'So you're impulsive, Sah-sha, umm, I must remember that,' he said, momentarily opening the one eye that was ice-free to study me before closing it again.

'No, just not very sensible when it comes to love, I think.

It was new to me… that sort of insane passion… it doesn't matter. It crashed and burned. His photographic talent was best fueled by drugs and you need money to buy drugs and you know the story.' My voice tapered off, I'm tired of talking about it now… enough.

I felt Nik's hands squeeze my hips. 'It gets easier,' he said.

'Got some experience in this?' I asked.

'Never been divorced, but we've all got our skeletons,' he said. 'You're special, Sah-sha.'

I laughed.

'But you can't take compliments,' he said and he pulled my hand and the ice away from his eye, he blinked open both eyes and looked at me.

'I think you're amazing,' he said. 'Shh…' he stopped me from interrupting him again. 'No denying it, no shrugging me off. I want you to say thank you, Niklas, you are right, I am amazing,' he teased me.

I bit my tongue between my teeth and made a face at him. 'That's not going to happen,' I said, 'and not because I'm insecure or have low self-esteem, I know exactly my strengths and weaknesses.'

'I know some of them too,' he said.

'Already? I doubt it,' I said, impatiently. *Yeah I'm so transparent that Nik can sum me up in a minute.*

'You're beautiful and trusting but you've had your wings clipped so now you're cautious and licking your wounds. You trust your family and close friends but you're not going to make the same mistakes again,' he said, watching me and not stopping for breath. 'You're ambitious and creative, you need very little company. You're a bit hyper and if you didn't design, work, exercise and do flips down your catwalk you would probably be clawing the roof. You want to make your own mark, you dress how you want to dress regardless of what people think, and you like me,' he finished with a grin to make it all less serious.

I smiled then bit my lip while I studied him and thought about what he said; he read me pretty well, I had to give him more credit for insight than I realized.

'Agree I've drawn you pretty well?' he asked.

'Maybe,' I told him. 'You on the other hand… you're a closed book. I know virtually nothing about you, your family or friends or what you want or why you decided to come here to the Saints.'

He shrugged. 'You'll have to spend some time with me then.'

I wriggled to a more comfortable position on his lap.

'Keep moving like that Sah-sha and I'll have to take matters into hand.'

'Huh,' I scoffed. *He wouldn't dare.* 'I still believe what I said to you before; if you want to survive this season with the Saints' you'd do best to avoid me.'

He leaned forward to kiss me but didn't account for my own super fast reflexes; I got that bag of ice in between us so fast he dropped back with a groan as the cold pressure touched his eye.

'You're killing me Sah-sha.'

'I know, I've been saying that all along.' I rolled my eyes.

*****

I had spent the last hour or so reading in bed, trying to relax my mind for sleep. I put my book down, slid under the sheets and turned off the bedside light.

I couldn't believe Adam would just arrive like that – seeing him always set me back, dropping me in all the pain again and I had to sort and re-file everything in my head. I sent Nik home empty-handed, the gun in his pants loaded and with a black eye. Not a great night for him, but hey, I didn't invite him over and I didn't want to celebrate my divorce night shagging some other guy; that's one memory I didn't need.

I had to stop thinking of Nik as a potential new guy on the scene, I seriously wasn't ready yet, I had other plans and I didn't need a relationship pulling me off course. It had taken a while, but Adam was out of my system – sure I slipped every now and then, but I knew what I needed and what the pain would be like if I relapsed into Adam's arms. There was no better deterrent than remembering that pain. Add to this I had a great job, I had my design business, good friends, and my wonderful apartment – hell, I was the poster girl for on track.

Then my phone beeped. It was nearly midnight. Who was messaging me at this hour? I reached for it and the room lit with the soft glow of the screen. Nik! Really?

NIK: Can't sleep, black eye. R U OK?

ME: Not playing Nik. Go find some nice safe girl. Over and out

NIK: Found girl, not interested in safe

ME: Girl worried for you and her

NIK: How about our Friday date? One step at a time

ME: I've got some friends I can set you up with

Then there was nothing. Well, that might have worked. Seriously, what was Nik's game? I knew he had plenty of girlfriends, so, was it just the challenge of getting one across the line that turned him down? Men, they are so – my phone beeped again – persistent.

NIK: Sasha, if you really don't like me, say so now and I'll go away

So there is an end point. A bloody nose and a hit to the eye didn't do it, but now if I said so Nik would go away. Excellent.

ME: Go away

NIK: You didn't say you didn't like me

ME: FUCK

NIK: Now?

ME: Goodnight, don't be late for the media call tomorrow

NIK: Yes Ma'am.

I just put the phone down and settled back in my sheets when it binged again. For the love of technology, shut up already. I reached out and grabbed the phone. It wasn't Nik this time, it was ex-hubby, Adam.

ADAM: You looked good tonight

ME: Thanks, you too

ADAM: Miss you

ME: Only cause you saw me tonight

ADAM: No. Often think of you

ME: Not doing this

ADAM: Can I come round?

ME: No. You are single, go spread your seed

ADAM: Fuck you, Sash, same as always

ME: You loved that once.

There was another quiet break. Maybe he was gone now too. I was on a roll tonight. *I'm bound to end up alone and living with the offspring of Prada – actually I'm okay with that.* I yawned. Maybe I should turn my phone off. Nope, there it was another text.

ADAM: Nite, Sash. I love you

An arrow hit my heart. I wish we could be like every other divorced couple and just hate each other.

ME: Nite Ad. I love you too. You are my favorite ex-hubby

And then I put the phone on silent and dropped back into bed. Six hours until morning.

Chapter 6

I had to bite the bullet and go and see The Russian – this wasn't going to be pretty. Given he was in charge of Saints' security and I had a media gathering today where Adam the ex-husband-photographer and Niklas the Saints' star recruit might both be present, *'Houston, we have a problem'* or could have one. *The Daily* said a photographer would be there, they couldn't say who. Of course Nik would be present in all his German glory, wearing his Saints' suit and glaring at me like I was the fish that tugged off his line and swam away. I wasn't sure Nik would restrain himself if he had a chance to return the favor to Adam and smack him in the head. Seriously when did my life become complicated again? I was doing so well only last week.

I rang *The Daily* again to see if they could confirm who they were sending but the pictorial editor was out. Damn him. I was just about to go in and see The Russian when Alice arrived. She gave me a glance which said she had seen Nik this morning.

'Morning Sash and Kay.' She dumped her gear and fell onto her chair. 'Okay, Sash, let's talk.'

I grimaced. *Here it comes.*

'What the hell did you do to my housemate now?' she asked.

Kay drew a sharp breath. 'Oh no, you didn't have to call the doctor again for Nik?'

I sighed. 'If Nik could get it into his big, handsome, German head that I'm not interested in men at the moment and stop dropping around to ask me out, he'd be a lot safer,' I said.

But wait there's more, it gets better, because then The Russian stomped into our office partition area – all imposing six-foot-five of him, blocking the light.

'Sasha, we need to talk,' his voice boomed. 'I just saw the Kaiser; you gave him a black eye?' I saw a hint of amusement in his eyes.

Yeah, ha ha. Kay and Alice gasped and my boss Jim appeared from around the corner on hearing all the chatter.

'Sasha couldn't even reach his eye,' Jim contributed.

I smiled gratefully. 'Thank you, boss, you're right, I didn't give him a black eye,' I said, as all heads turned back to look at me. 'It's complicated. I've told Nik it's better for his health to stay away but do you think he listens? No, he dropped in and so did my ex-husband who just became my ex – he was delivering the divorce papers and he took a swing at Nik because my ex is a dickhead, then bolted so luckily Nik didn't open fire, but I wasn't expecting either of them.' I stopped for breath.

'You've been married before?' Alice said.

Before I got a chance to cover that base, The Russian spoke up. He shook his head. 'Right, I'm going to have to ban him from going near you.'

'Yes, please, that would be great,' I said.

'You can't stand in the way of true love, Russian,' Kay contributed, picking up her tea and sipping it as though she was in the middle of watching a soap opera.

'I agree,' Alice added, 'you ban Nik from being near Sasha and all you will achieve is making Sasha more desirable to him.'

'True,' Jim piped in, 'you always want what you can't have until you get it, and then it's not such a big deal.'

'Hello,' I said, aloud, 'I'm sitting here! I'm not a German Wiener that Nik's craving.' I shook my head.

'Wiener, that's a sausage isn't it?' Kay asked.

I sighed. 'Russian, tell him to stay away, Kay it's not true love and yes it is a sausage, Alice, there's plenty of groupies out there for Nik, and boss, I'm going to go over and prepare for the media conference.'

I heard Jim chuckling as I rose, grabbed my press kits, and departed to the media room where we held a media briefing before home game days. It was in the building next door and let me escape for a while so they could all talk about true love and sausages without me present. I hadn't given The Russian the full picture and I would have to do that sooner rather than later. The media conferences ran for about forty-five minutes at the most and the coach Johan spoke along with a few of the players. It was great for me because I didn't have to set up ten separate interview times.

I arrived at the room in the adjoining building, unlocked the room, turned on the lights, cleaned the table at the front of the room and stuck four chairs behind it. I put out some water glasses and a jug, propped the press kits near the door and looked around. That was pretty much all that needed to be done. Usually three or four players were required to the pre-game day press conferences so the media could have access to them including Captain Lucas who had to be there; they were rostered on to attend by Shayne and I knew Nik was one of them this week. I opened a few of the windows and pulled back blinds to let the natural light in. I glanced out through the window to the parking lot and saw Nik's SUV. He was here – probably inside showing everyone his bruised eye and getting sympathy, poor baby. Next to his VW was Captain Lucas's Lamborghini and I recognized our midfielder Josh's Audi. Good, I like the boys to be here before the media and not keep them waiting.

I heard a noise and wheeled around. Nik was standing in the entrance way. My hand went straight to my heart. 'You scared the hell out of me,' I said, breathing out.

He smiled and walked towards me. His eyes were alight with interest, his smile gorgeous and he walked with the confident air of a man who had it all – it was a heady mix. Not to mention that man could wear a suit – the Saints' uniform was cut to perfection on him. Yep I'd like to take that inside leg measurement. Hold up, I didn't just say that... focus.

'Hello Sah-sha, miss me? I've missed you,' he teased me with an engaging smile. Was that a dimple? No, not fair.

I held my hands up and ordered him to stop.

'Don't come a step closer, Niklas,' I warned him. He stopped on the spot; it constantly surprised me how good he was at following orders.

Nik held up his hands in frustration and looked around. 'What could go wrong now?'

I shook my head. 'You've got a game this Sunday, we're not tempting fate,' I said. 'You look very... presentable by the way.'

Nik grinned, that beautiful white teeth grin from his lovely tanned face surrounded by his gorgeous blond hair... I'd love to slip my tongue between his lips.

'Presentable? That's a new one for me,' he said. 'And you Sah-sha look delectable,' he said, the word rolling off his tongue with his German lilt. 'I love that dress on you.'

'Thanks,' I said, looking everywhere but at him. I was wearing a lightweight crepe, long-sleeved red dress to below my knees with black leather boots. Not one of my own designs but one of my personal faves that I had whipped up from a Vogue pattern. I had a matching black velvet bowler hat in the office. He walked a step towards me and I stepped back, hitting the desk. 'Not a step further,' I warned him.

The Russian walked in. 'I agree, Kaiser, didn't we just have that chat?'

Bless you Russian, you're worth every cent today, not most days, but today, yes.

Nik turned his blue eyes to The Russian. I think they changed from passionate to blazing.

'Yes we did Russian, now fuck off,' he said.

Mm, this wasn't going as well as I thought. The Russian smirked.

'Come on, Nik, it's for your own safety,' The Russian said using his name instead of his nickname to indicate the seriousness of the situation, I'm guessing. He put a hand on Nik's shoulder and Nik flinched and moved away. The Russian held his hands up in a peace gesture. What's that about? The man looked as though he didn't mind being touched last night when he wanted me on his lap.

'If you want to talk to Sasha, you'll need to carry a first aid kit,' The Russian joked. 'We had an agreement.' The Russian was taking this security stuff seriously.

'I told you I'd do my best not to thump the ex-husband, but I need to talk to Sah-sha,' Nik said, staring at me with a look that said he was hungry.

'I'm really sorry about your eye,' I said, again, looking at the dark bruising. 'Maybe you shouldn't be here; you're going to get questions about it.'

'It's fine,' he said and came another step towards me.

'Actually, after the ambulance statement we had to put out earlier this week, I'm thinking you're too risky to have at this press conference now that you've got the black eye as well. I should have thought of that first thing this morning,' I said, my stress levels rising. I held my hand up for them both to wait and I quickly pressed a direct dial number in my contacts.

Nik shook his head and crossed his arms across his lovely suited chest.

'Sorry buddy,' The Russian was saying to him.

'Shayne, it's Sasha, oh good,' I hung up.

'What was that?' Nik asked and I pointed to the door where Shayne had just walked into the media room. He was in the suit pants and a white shirt, carrying the tie and jacket. The media would be arriving in about fifteen minutes and he had to set a good example.

'What's up Sash?' Shayne asked, putting his phone back in his pocket and slipping on his jacket; he was always so supportive. 'Hi boys,' he said taking in The Russian and Nik. Then he saw it. 'Fuck Nik, what happened to your eye?'

'Um, he might have run into my 'ex's' fist. I think he should leave,' I added quickly, 'especially since we had to release a statement from the doctor about his health on Monday night.'

Nik looked as though he'd be ganged up on. 'I'm rostered to be here, it's not like I requested it… I had to come off the beach, shave and get changed.'

'I know and I really appreciate you coming, I do, but…' I said, and looked to Shayne for his thoughts.

'For real?' Nik said, looking from me to Shayne to The Russian. 'Every one of us is sporting different injuries every week, we're professional athletes.'

'Yeah, but a black eye begs a few questions,' I said.

'Sash is right,' Shayne said, 'it's risky.'

'Oh for fuck's sake, you've got to be kidding,' Nik said, turning his attention back to me as though the decision was all mine. Then Doc arrived early. He was on hand to answer any player fitness queries if Johan the coach asked him to do so. The Doc came up to us and addressed Nik.

'How are you feeling since Monday?' and then he saw Nik's black eye. 'What the… that wasn't there Monday was it?' He looked at me.

Nik threw up his hands.

'Stay still,' Doc ordered him as he studied Nik's face. Nik brushed him off and glared at me with a look that had nothing to do with undressing this time. I shrugged apologetically.

A camera crew strode in behind us and Shayne winced seeing them. 'Too late now, you'll have to stay Nik.' He nudged our group together. 'Okay, so it's just an injury from last weekend's game, right? Unless your 'ex' is likely to say something?'

I saw the Doc's eyes widen as he took in the reason for the black eye. Crap, all this shit was not good for my career at the Saints.

I shook my head. 'I don't know for sure that *The Daily* is sending him, but he won't do anything stupid while he's working,' I said, and silently prayed to the god of idiot men that he wouldn't make me a liar.

'Nik, keep a low profile,' Shayne ordered. 'Russian, keep him out of trouble…'

Nik went to protest and Shayne held up his hand and kept talking, 'Sash, you stay on the opposite side of the room from Nik, just to be safe.'

'Right,' I said. 'Oh crap.' I looked to the door where my 'ex', Adam entered with his camera gear and a journalist from *The Daily*. Nik arced up, I literally saw him expand by about three or four inches and not where you think.

'That him?' The Russian asked and I nodded, placing my hand on Nik's arm.

'Who?' Doc said, trying to catch up. He and Shayne turned to look.

'Sasha's ex-husband who took a quick shot at Nik last night and gave him the black eye, then bolted before he copped it,' The Russian finished.

'Well done, big mouth,' I said, and frowned at The Russian whose lips turned up slightly in a smile. He was one of the girls, our Russian, loved to be amongst the gossip.

Shayne ran his hand through his hair. 'Just gets better. Nik... hey, Nik!' he snapped, trying to get his attention.

'Shayne?' Nik frowned and turned to look at him.

'Not one foot in that guy's direction, do you understand me?' Shayne ordered. 'He's not worth getting a charge over, or missing out on the weekend game. Understood?'

Nik nodded, returning his gaze to Adam, his eyes narrowing. The two locked looks and I saw Adam smile. *Fucking fantastic, just what I need.*

Nik stepped towards him and the wall that was The Russian blocked him.

'Get him out of here and hurry,' Shayne ordered and The Russian got a hand around the back of Nik's neck, keeping it friendly-looking, and directed him to a different exit to where the media was entering. Both men were tall but The Russian had a lot more weight behind him and the element of surprise with the speedy block.

The Russian got Nik clear of the room in time and I watched the two argue as The Russian walked Nik to his car.

I breathed a sigh of relief and looked around to see Shayne watching over my shoulder. Doc had wandered towards the media to distract them from the circus we were staging behind them.

'We've paid a lot of money for that guy, Sash, don't corrupt him,' Shayne said, sort of joking but not really.

I sighed. 'Shayne, honestly I've got a lot on my plate and I haven't been encouraging Nik at all, he's not even on my radar.'

'I know, I believe that, but that's probably made you more interesting to him,' Shayne said.

Again with the can't-have theory.

We watched from the window as Nik shrugged The Russian's arm off him, and he unlocked his car and got in.

Shayne cleared his throat. 'I don't know Nik that well yet, but he doesn't have a lot of people in his life and he doesn't let too many in from what the guys have said. If he clicks with you, I'm guessing he thinks that's worth pursuing.'

'I don't get why; we've met a few times in the office and I took him to a media interview once, that's it. There's no shortage of girls after these guys. You know all about it.' I stated the obvious to Shayne an ex-player. 'Where is his family? He's cagey about that.'

'He has none, well none that he's declared. His next of kin on his contract is his financial manager,' Shayne said, 'but keep that to yourself.'

'Wow,' I said. We watched him drive out of the grounds.

'Can you dial-him-a date or something?' I asked Shayne, tongue in cheek.

Shayne chuckled. 'Leave it with me. I'll call Babes-R-Us.'

We both grinned and got back to the business of the media conference as everyone began to arrive.

Chapter 7

Before I left work I messaged Nik to apologize about the press conference earlier and he messaged me back to say no big deal and asked again about Friday night, sigh. I let that one slide. I was meeting my brother Ethan, my best friend Max and his partner Ren for a post-work drink. We made a bit of a habit of doing it every Wednesday night. I was closer to Ethan than my other brothers, not just in looks but we just got on; maybe because our personalities were nothing alike – being a counselor, Ethan was calm and considerate, rational and thoughtful. I was none of those things. Max and Ren didn't always come but Ethan and I never missed beer and burger night at the local hotel. They were all there when I arrived.

'What the fuck?' I said. 'Is my watch slow? People keep arriving everywhere before me, it's as though I'm in the Twilight Zone.'

'Hi Sassy,' Ethan said, grinning. He rose, kissed me on the cheek and I leaned over to kiss Max and Ren while we were doing the kiss thing.

'But seriously, what time do you have Maxie?' I asked.

'Two minutes past six,' he answered. Ren looked at his watch. 'I've got five past.' Ethan followed suit. 'Five to the hour here.'

I shook my head. 'Synchronized then, good.' The boys laughed.

'I love that outfit on you Sass, red is you and cute little bowler hat,' Ren said.

'Thanks Ren, it's just something I whipped up.' I smiled at him. 'How are you?' I asked, studying him. Both he and Max were thin; Ren was the geeky type who looked as though a gust of wind would knock him over while Max was solid and tall but pretty, preened to within an inch of his life like you'd expect from any self-respecting hairdresser. Before Ren could answer Max stepped in answering for his boyfriend.

'He's in a green smoothie stage,' Max said, with a roll of his eyes. 'Awful. Every time I turn around there's a celery stick and a broccoli bunch heading towards the blender.'

'That sounds wonderfully healthy,' my brother encouraged Ren.

'I try, God knows I try,' Ren said. 'Every time I start a new health phase they change the rules about what's healthy. Meat was in then out, potatoes were fine but then too starchy, garlic is good for warding off colds, but it wards off friends too... it's not easy.'

'I really liked it when you were going through the chocolate fondue stage,' Max said.

I laughed. I loved these boys. I kind of had Alice lined

up for my brother Ethan before she fell for Tomás, but there was no way she'd even notice my darling brother now, even if he was cute and charming – a bit like Ryan Gosling, only younger and prettier – okay, nothing like him at all. I grabbed the waiter's attention. We all ordered the same thing we ordered every week and then I turned to Ethan.

'How goes work?' I asked.

'Tough week.' Ethan exhaled. We really did look more like twins than Saffron and me. He ran his hand through his short blond hair and gave me a tired smile.

'I couldn't do what you do.' Ren shook his head. 'I take my hat off to you bro.'

'Thanks, yeah, it can be tough. This week, was just the usual court-appointed clients, but I tell you, I had this guy today who had beaten his wife to the point that she had to hospitalized and he couldn't understand what he'd done wrong,' Ethan said, and shook his head. 'He said it was her fault for not having dinner ready when he got home.'

'You've got to wonder what happened in his childhood and family life, to make him like that,' I said, squeezing my brother's arm. We had such a great childhood that all my mistakes were truly my own doing.

'Exactly,' he agreed with me. 'Then I get the other extreme today… a teenager who has been abused by his father for years and now he's been expelled from school for bad behavior. Go figure.'

'Do you still like it, what you do?' I asked, 'because you could take a break and do some modeling or do relationship counseling or something a bit easier.'

Ethan scoffed, 'Are you offering me a job on your catwalk? Nah, my college modeling days are over, but it's all fine. I always wanted to work in this area, it's just some days you've got to go and find something good in order to remember that this crap isn't the norm.'

Our drinks arrived and we clinked our glasses in a toast.

'I'll tell you something good,' Max said, 'a group of Saints has just walked in. Know them, Sassy?'

I cringed and turned around slowly. *Man, can't I go out without running into the team after hours?* I breathed a sigh of relief; it was only a few of the guys, they must live locally – I recognized Harry and Jackson, but they moved out of sight quickly, disappearing around the corner following the waitress who was seating them.

'God they're hot,' Ren said.

'So hot,' Max agreed. 'You'll be like that if you keep up that green smoothie diet.'

'Think so?' Ren said, looking at his biceps.

Ethan and I grinned at each.

'Ah love, ain't it grand?' I said, admiring the two of them.

'Speaking of which, how's the love life?' Ethan asked me.

'Funny you should ask,' I said. 'I have a German stalker… from the Saints.'

'Not the Kaiser?' Max asked.

'Since when did you follow soccer?' I frowned at him.

'Since you started working for them,' he said. 'Don't say I'm not a supportive best friend. He just came in you know.'

I flipped around again but couldn't see him. 'Are you sure?' I asked.

'I'd know him anywhere,' Max said, and Ren nodded.

My eyes narrowed. 'Did he have a girl with him?' I asked.

Max shook his head. 'He was with those other Saints.' Max got distracted. 'There's a friend of mine, James, I'll be back.' Max and Ren excused themselves and I looked towards the area that the Saints were shown to. I couldn't see Nik and I wondered if he saw me.

'Sassy—' Ethan started.

'Oh no,' I stopped him, 'I recognize that tone. I'm going to get the 'get back on the horse' lecture aren't I?' I said, narrowing my eyes at him. 'Is this my brother or my therapist talking?'

Ethan webbed his fingers together and leaned forward. 'Both. Sass, you need to trust in love again.'

I rolled my eyes. 'What a lovely notion,' I said.

Ethan grabbed my hand. 'No really. I know we've spoken of this before, but when you met Adam, you were pretty naive and he was your first major love. So you bought into it, you believed he was going to be loyal and it would be happily ever after…'

'I blame our parents for being such great role models,' I mumbled, sipping my drink.

Ethan grinned. 'Yeah, damn them. But not all guys are like your ex-husband; some of us believe in commitment and loyalty, so don't give up on that, okay? That's all I'm saying.'

'Sure that's all you're saying?' I narrowed my eyes and Ethan laughed.

'Well I wouldn't mind adding a bit about the fact that Adam is unlikely to change, ever, but you'll know what is right next time because your eyes are wide open.'

'If there's a next time,' I said.

'Sass, there'll be a next time. You deserve love and you deserve someone who believes in it as you do. Don't let this experience harden you, take a chance.'

I went to brush Ethan off again but he knew me too well.

'For me?'

I groaned. 'You're not going to play that card are you?'

Ethan nodded. 'I am. Take a chance for me because seeing you happy would bring a lot of happiness into my world. Try?' he said.

I didn't answer and he nudged his foot against mine under the table. I nodded sort of and he smiled.

'I'll take that as a yes. Let the man in,' Ethan said. 'You got to remember he's had some experience too and his heart might not be whole either.'

I scoffed. 'He told me he's never been turned down, ever.'

'That doesn't mean that he's found what he wants,' Ethan said.

Chapter 8

I had had company or gone out nearly every night since the weekend, so I decided Thursday night was my designated stay home with Prada night. The music was pumping and I was pushing through my sit-ups in sets of twenty, then to the push-ups which I didn't manage quite as well, back to the weights set and then the skipping. I had my twenty-five minute circuit worked out and my music tracks timed perfectly for them.

I finished and panting, I ventured to the kitchen for water. I loved the feeling after a workout, when the mind and body were relaxed. I did some of my best thinking when I worked out. Even Prada got into it with a few stretches before deciding he was svelte enough and returning to his bird-watching post.

I showered, dressed and spent an hour getting a head start on cutting Saffy's wedding dress. I was on fire tonight – I could achieve so much when I was boyfriend-less. Tick that box, right, then I headed to the kitchen, grabbed a glass of wine and made my way to the sofa. It wasn't the best diet, so maybe I'd have some toast later. While enjoying my wine, watching *Outlander*, in the company of a beautiful male… cat – the love of my life, I realized I hadn't heard from Nik since the return text after the press conference or Adam since he told me by text that he loved me. Fuck you, Adam and Nik. Life sucked sometimes – I was perfectly happy before Nik decided that he needed to be in my life, now I just had to remember that. Either he really was shitty at me about the press conference or he saw me sitting with my hand on Ethan's arm.

I kind of missed hearing from him, damn him… damn men, but I wasn't going to make contact. I told him I wasn't ready and it was best he stayed away for his own safety and now he was doing that, I would just have to accept it. Maybe he had just decided to let it go, which was a good thing, even though I felt flat. See, this is why you shouldn't start these things. It creates a space and then you've got to fill it.

Getting over Adam was easier… seeing him flirting with one of the journos at my Saints' press conference brought back all the drama he caused me and there had been plenty of it – cheating, lies, snorting drugs and there had been plenty of great sex too – I wish the sex was bad; it would make it so much easier to forget him.

My phone rang and I debated whether to tear myself away from watching *Outlander* – I'd love to personally fit that kilt that Jamie wears, he was so manly yet vulnerable, sexy and – where was I? Oh yeah, or just ignore my phone. Ah, the pull was too strong. I went to the counter and grabbed it. It was my 'bestie' Max.

'Hi Maxie,' I answered, taking the opportunity to top up my chardonnay while in the kitchen. I returned to sit next to Prada.

'Babe,' he said, 'so what's happening with the German?'

I sighed. 'Nothing. We were jinxed. I warned him to stay away for his own safety and it looks like that worked.'

'Why would you do that?' Max's voice went up an octave.

'Because I'm an idiot.'

'Oh, right then,' Max said, agreeing.

'Because it is too soon. I've just got into a really good space, I like that space,' I said.

'I understand but major bummer on the timing,' Max said.

I shrugged, not that Max could see that on the phone. 'It's a good thing, really,' I said. 'I didn't mention this last night in front of Ethan, but Adam dropped in the divorce papers earlier this week and Nik was here. There was an incident.'

I heard Max sigh and he dropped his voice as though someone else was in the room with him. 'Fucking Adam, I'm sorry Sassy, but I'm glad he's out of your life. That boy was nothing but trouble. Ooh, I sounded like your father then... not the fucking part; I don't think I've ever heard him swear.'

I asked after Ren and we chatted for a bit, before hanging up. I unpaused *Outlander* and watched for ten minutes before my phone pinged with a text. I flicked the screen, and saw the text was from Alice.

ALICE: what have you done to my housemate?

I rolled my eyes. What the fuck? Anything that has happened to Nik now is not my fault; I haven't seen him since the press conference.

ME: Can't take credit for any recent injuries

ALICE: He's morose. Been so since Wed night

Mm, I thought back to last night and dinner with Ethan, Max and Ren. I wonder if he saw us. I texted Alice back.

ME: Define morose?

ALICE: Polite but not talking. Plays with the console non-stop. Not eating

ME: Prada was like that once, off his food. He had a furball

ALICE: Ha ha, I'm serious

Great, what does that mean? It might not even be about me… he might have had bad sex or be fighting with a groupie for godsake.

ME: What could it be?

ALICE: You know what it is. Do you really not like him?

Here we go. I won't get any work done if a guy enters my life, although I guess if it is Nik he's away playing every second weekend. But then I'd be going out with a player – how cliché and incestuous when I'm working there, I'll lose all credibility. Plus I've got to focus on Saffy's dress and now the mother-in-law's dress and I need to make a new hat for the wedding – hell yeah, that will take some time. He'd be good in bed though, I can imagine that strong, muscular tanned body, those arms that could hold themselves over me, and I've felt the imprint of his erection already… that was memorable.

The room was getting hotter. My phone pinged again.

ALICE: Hello?

ME: I like him a lot

ALICE: Then what's the problem?

ME: It's me

ALICE: Yeah we all know that. So get over it :)

ME: Thanks

ALICE: What's the worst that could happen?

I could have a broken heart again; spend weeks in agony; have to go underground to lick my wounds; leave town to get away from seeing, hearing or reading about him; have to give up my job… the list is endless.

ME: A lot

ALICE: What's the best that could happen?

I could have some great sex if he's capable in the sack; I could enjoy some great eye candy; maybe a bit of company beside Prada; get my family and friends off my back about getting back on the horse; have some fun; put Adam well and truly behind me; have a date for my sister's wedding besides Maxie… and maybe, just maybe, fall in love.

It did kind of weigh up pretty evenly both ways.

ME: OK

ALICE: OK, you'll contact him?

ME: Yes

ALICE: Fabo Sash. Can you do it ASAP?

ME: OK. Can you make sure he eats and drinks?

ALICE: Deal! Call him now, tonight?

ME: OK

I took another sip of chardonnay and drew a deep breath. I thought about what to say. 'Hi' and 'How are you?' seemed pretty lame, 'Want to see my catwalk?' sounded a bit suggestive, something nice wouldn't work, he knew me enough already to be suspicious about that. So I sent him a message.

ME: Still shitty with me about the press conference?

Yep, that covered it nicely, the last of the romantics… watch out Shakespeare, this girl could turn a verse. Then I waited. What if he didn't text back now and Alice was wrong? Fucking fantastic, I'd look like a dickhead who doesn't know my own mind. I sighed, this is the problem with relationships – I just want something direct and easy without all the coding and deciphering required. My phone beeped and I reached for it with speed and hesitancy if you can imagine how that works. It was from Nik.

NIK: Not shitty with you. Thinking of me, huh?

ME: Yep

I'm going for the direct approach, we were both okay at that from the small window of experience we had communicating together.

NIK: Where's the boyfriend?

Ah there it was. He did see me – given how direct he normally is you'd think he'd just ask. But maybe he didn't think I'd be honest. Why?

ME: What boyfriend?

NIK: Wed night at hotel?

ME: My brother, best friend and his guy?

There was a temporary lull in communications. This was interesting… then the phone pinged again.

NIK: Can I come over now?

ME: Yep

That was it. A few minutes later the phone beeped again and it was Alice this time.

ALICE: You are the best. Nik now up
ME: How up?
ALICE: You tell me ;) See you at work tomorrow xx

*****

Nik must have hired a Learjet because he was at my door in about twenty minutes, showered, smelling delicious and earning that nickname the Kaiser – the emperor in English – oh yeah, conquer me, Nik. Wow, how fickle was I? One minute I'm saying stay away, the next I'm opening my front door to a gorgeous German man. Clearly I am only human and here I was thinking I was above humanity, sigh. He wore jeans, a white T-shirt which made his blue eyes really stand out and a navy jacket.

We stood looking at each other for just a few moments. I confess the feeling of relief and excitement seeing him there in the flesh swept over me. I hated that. Thank God he arrived quickly before I had time to analyze myself and the situation to death – phew. Did I mention he looked gorgeous?

I smiled and stood aside and he entered. I closed the door and when I turned around he was right next to me, only inches from me. He pulled me the final few inches closer and rested his chin on my head, wrapping his arms around me. I hesitated for a minute, and then my arms wove inside his coat and around him. He was all muscle. I tried not to feel him up.

I felt him exhale and he stayed there for a few minutes as if he was losing the tension of the day and drawing strength from me. He pulled away, leaned down and then his lips found mine. It was so sensual. His hand moved behind my neck and into my hair and he pressed against me, his lips touching mine with softness and passion. Holy fuck, this was good, very good. Then he pulled away and looked me in the eyes with his beautiful crystal blue eyes.

'Sah-sha.'

'Niklas.'

He smiled, a dimple appearing on his tanned face. Damn, he was a beautiful man, I could design an entire fashion line around him and I might – I'll call it the Kaiser!

'I knew you would come around,' he teased me. 'I was waiting for you to make the next move, but then I thought maybe you had a guy.' He released me, slipped his navy jacket off and placed it with his keys on the entrance table.

'Mm, waiting on me huh?' I said, 'What if I didn't make contact?'

'I would have died,' he said, teasing me.

My hand went to my heart. 'Thank God I messaged you.'

He grinned and followed me as I walked into the kitchen to offer him a drink. I knew he wouldn't have alcohol with the game this weekend.

'Niklas you are so very smooth,' I said. 'Dying for unrequited love, how romantic and all this time I thought the French and Italians were the true romantics, not the Germans.'

He shook his head. 'So wrong. No spin, I'm not into it but I'm into you, Sah-sha. I always know what I want straight up, always have.'

I studied him. 'Lucky you. There's always been gray areas for me. Will you have a cola or a juice or coffee?'

'Coffee thanks.'

'White with none,' I said.

Nik smiled. 'How romantic, Sah-sha, you remembered. What else do you remember about me? Sitting on my lap?'

'Um.' I flicked the kettle on and looked towards the ceiling as I thought. 'I remember you bleeding all over my guest sofa and holding ice to your black eye and…'

'Right,' he sighed, 'happy memories.'

I folded my arms across my chest and leaned against the kitchen island. 'So Mr. Black-and-white, you're telling me that with all the friends you've met since arriving here late last year, and all the sex you've had…' he went to deny it and I cut him off, '… you're a single player, c'mon on…' His eyes narrowed as he waited for me to finish and I continued: 'Do you mean to say that you haven't found anyone yet that you knew you wanted straight away… no spark?'

'You're fishing so I can say you are the only one,' he read me.

'Yes and no,' I said. Two can play at direct. 'I want to understand why you know you want this, it's not like we've had a great start.' I reached for a cup, put coffee in and pulled the milk from the fridge.

His tongue briefly appeared between his clenched teeth as he thought, then he used it to lick his lower lip and he swallowed. *Fuck that was sexy. I have to think of more hard questions to ask so I can see that again.*

'I just connected with you, from the start… there was something,' he said. 'You're different, you're full of energy and you do your own thing, have your own style. That's the best way I can describe it.'

'I think it was just an electric shock from the carpet in the office,' I reminded him. 'What if you're wrong?'

'Then I'm wrong,' he said. 'But I'm not.' He went to reach for me and I pushed him away.

'Boiling water,' I said, making his coffee. 'Just stay clear, not worth the risk.'

He shook his head at me.

'I learned something about you before the press conference,' I said.

I noticed Nik stiffen… what did he think I was going to say?

'What's that?' he tried to say casually but his eyes gave him away.

'I noticed you are not six-foot-five like your player sheet and stats online says. You were standing next to The Russian and you were a couple of inches shorter,' I said, raising an eyebrow in his direction.

Nik visibly relaxed and breathed out. He smiled at me. 'Shayne got it wrong on the stats sheet when he was doing all my early profile stuff… translation problem.'

'Uh-huh,' I said, suspiciously. 'And why haven't we fixed it?'

Nik grinned before answering. 'Because Lucas and the boys wanted to leave it… it cheeses The Russian off – he likes to think he's the tallest in the club.'

I smiled and shook my head. 'You guys are so competitive. So what are you?'

'Six-foot-three, plenty big enough,' he said, suggestively.

I bit my lower lip as I stopped to study him and gave him just the hint of a nod.

'I'm changing it,' I said.

'Spoilsport.' He took the coffee from me and thanked me. 'You look very cute. You have a good body,' he said, his gaze traveling over the black leggings and black hoodie I had changed into after my workout. My white socked feet were probably the highlight.

I laughed. 'You're so direct. Well, Nik, you have a good body too.'

'Want to see it?' he asked.

More than you'll ever know buddy, but I didn't say that. I smiled at him. 'Have you eaten?'

'I wasn't hungry before.'

'Crap, Nik, bad, very bad,' I scolded him, 'you've got to eat, you can't train the amount you do if you're not balancing your diet. The coach and Doc would kick your butt if they knew that you haven't eaten, then kick mine.'

He shrugged. 'It was a disrupted week.'

I sighed. 'I know, I'm sorry after the nosebleed incident, and the punch, and the eviction from the press conference.'

'The waves weren't good either,' he said, with the hint of a smile. 'But that wasn't your fault.' He moved closer to me again and this time I let him. There was this weird current running between us. I swear all my hairs were standing on end. He put a hand either side of me on the counter and looked down at me. 'Sah-sha, I would take a black eye for you any day as long as I was your boyfriend.'

I smiled up at him. Tall, all that muscle, tough on the

ground, gentle in bed – allegedly – and so sure of what he wants. I'm not sure I've met anyone like Nik.

'I don't want you ever taking a hit for me Nik. Now focus, the rest of the team would have eaten the equivalent to a small Italian village in pasta by now – you have to eat, have to have some protein and carbohydrates,' I said, giving him a lecture.

'I'm feeling hungrier now,' he agreed. 'See, you're good for me already. Have you eaten?'

'I had a liquid dinner,' I said, nodding towards the remaining chardonnay in my glass.

He frowned. 'Not good enough. Come on, we'll go get something.'

'I have ingredients here, we can cook,' I said. 'Homemade will be better for you.' I went to my pantry and pulled out some whole-wheat pasta, a tin of tomato paste and pointed to the fridge and freezer, directing Nik to get the ground beef, fresh tomatoes and herbs. We got to work.

'You have a lot in your freezer for a single person,' Nik said, with just a hint of suspicion in his voice.

How can someone that gorgeous and successful be so insecure?

'I have three brothers and a male best friend,' I reminded him. 'Every time they drop in, they just happen to be hungry, so I'm well-stocked.'

We cooked next to each other and I set aside some beef for Prada even though he had eaten. Nik diced fresh tomatoes and herbs that were donated to the kitchen by Max's mom. I did the pan work on the hot stove plate, safer that way… it was bad enough giving Nik a sharp knife in my presence.

'Your brother, is that the one you had your hand on?' he asked, in between sips of his coffee.

Ah, so he did see that.

'That's him. That's Ethan,' I said. 'You should have come over and I would have introduced you.'

'I thought that might be uncomfortable for you if he was your boyfriend. Do your brothers look like triplets?' Nik asked.

'Two look really alike – Jason and Sam. They look like Saffron, with the dark hair and brown eyes. Ethan and I look similar,' I said. 'We're close.' I cast a glance towards Nik.

'Tell me about your family,' I pushed him again. He went to open his mouth and I jumped in. 'And don't say there's nothing to tell… I've told you about mine, you have to give now.'

'Can I have a glass of water?' he stalled.

'Of course. I've got juice too, so help yourself to whatever you want from the fridge.' I reached for a tall glass and gave it to him. It was nice cooking beside him in the kitchen; I was acutely aware of the space he filled and I knew he felt it too. He forgot his train of thought each time he came within inches of me. Or he was in fear of his life… whichever.

He filled up a glass with water, gulped some down and returned to stirring the beef while I boiled the pasta. I waited, not really patiently and tried hard not to ask the question again.

'This is ready, I think Sah-sha,' he said, putting some ground beef on the wooden spoon for me to taste. I tried it and agreed.

'I have to do the pasta test,' I said. With a fork, I picked out a strand of pasta from the boiling pot of water and threw it against the kitchen splash-back tiles. The pasta stuck there.

'What the fuck?' Nik laughed, surprised.

'It's ready,' I said, 'that's how you can tell.'

'Right,' he said, and laughed again.

I grabbed two bowls and drained the pasta, directing him to the cutlery and napkins; he seemed to remember from our noodle night.

Still no talk of his family – what's that about?

I dished up a massive serve for him and a medium serve for me. I sprinkled grated fresh cheese on top, put Prada's bowl of beef on the kitchen floor and we moved to sit in the lounge on the sofa – I never ate at the table, oh yeah, that's because I didn't have one.

'This is great,' Nik said, alternating between his glass of water and the pasta. 'Thank you, Sah-sha.'

'My pleasure. Now if you have a bad training session tomorrow it's got nothing to do with me,' I said, wiping my hands of all responsibility. 'So Nik, why don't you tell me something about your family? What's going on? Think I don't notice that you haven't shared?'

He continued to eat and attempted to look out the window, but could see only a bit of the night sky and the room reflected through the partially opened blinds.

'I have no family,' he said.

I nodded. 'No family still alive or no family you want to speak of?'

'I'm a Waise, um, an orphan,' he translated the German word.

I felt a wave of sadness for Nik; here was I talking about being from a big family – both parents who loved me, a twin with a special bond and three brothers, and Nik was alone in the world. I didn't push it any further.

'Lucky you met me and I have a big family then,' I said, 'we might just have to adopt you.'

He smiled and looked at me for the first time since the discussion started. I began to think Nik was a lot more complex than I first thought and I was going to scratch below that hunky surface gradually.

*****

To my surprise Nik didn't suggest he'd stay the night; I guess all his gear was at home and he had to be at training early. Maybe he thought he had to tread a little slow and if he tried it on I'd pull back... I'm not sure I would. But he did help with the dishes.

'I'm glad you messaged me,' he said taking a plate from me and wiping it.

'Me too,' I said, 'I didn't realize how hungry I was.'

Nik gave me a smile and flicked the tea towel across my butt. 'So your brother and these friends you were with the other night, just friends, no boyfriend hiding under your bed?' he said, with a glance upstairs.

I rolled my eyes at him. 'No boyfriend,' I assured him. I saw his lip curl slightly in a smile. I suspect Nik was thinking he was back in the game and I was feeling pretty glad he was and freaked out too.

'What about you, Nik,' I dried my hands and turned to

face him. 'You go out after the game and I know you pick up. Anyone that you've had back for seconds?'

He looked a little confused.

'Anyone that you've been seeing regularly,' I clarified.

'No. After a game it's good to wind down with the team, especially when we win. I don't stay too late though, it's a long day.'

'Yeah but don't you usually head home from the bar with someone?' I asked, teasing him. 'I can't reveal my sources but someone I know overheard some ladies talking at the bar and they said you were a 'sensitive lover',' I said, making quote marks in the air and not telling on Alice who heard the convo. Lucky she told me before Nik and I hooked up because she wouldn't have spilled that otherwise.

I wonder what sensitive means? I hope he's manly, I like them manly – I don't want any lover crying after an orgasm for godsake!

He hesitated to answer. 'I won't be going home with anyone if I'm with you, Sah-sha. I think you are determined to think the worst of me.'

His words stopped me. I watched his mouth, his beautiful mouth usher those words with just a tightening of his lips as though my thoughts of him were undeserved. Was I doing that, looking for his faults and failures so I could make excuses to pull away from him? That's sort of what Ethan said too, as if I'm always looking out for an out.

'It not that, it's okay, I know players are players,' I said, taking the towel from him as we finished.

'I'm not a player if I'm in a relationship.'

'Okay,' I said, 'well when you're in a relationship you can behave.'

He pulled me close again. 'You're pushing me away again. I'm not a player in a relationship, Sah-sha.' He said it more slowly this time.

I looked away. Nik was always so direct that he caught me off guard sometimes. I didn't always have reactions prepared. He lifted my chin to make me look him in the eyes.

'Do you understand what I'm saying about us?' he said.

I nodded.

'Good. I have to go.' He leaned down to kiss me again. This time his tongue ventured in between my lips ever so slightly and I felt my breathing hitch. Fuck this man was hot and I was way too vulnerable for this.

He moved away and breathed out. 'You're a trouble maker, Sah-sha.' He shook his head at me. 'Now I have a huge erection,' he said, matter-of-factly.

I laughed as he broke the tension. 'It appears you do,' I agreed looking down at the tight press in his jeans.

'At least I am still in one piece. Good night, meine Süsse.'

'What does that mean?' I asked, my eyes narrowing with suspicion.

'My sweetie or sweetheart,' he said, with a cheeky look. He went to the table, grabbed his jacket, and put it on.

'I don't think I've ever been called sweet or...' I tried pronouncing it, 'sues-sza.'

'Good. Then it is my unique name for you. Unless we go to Germany and everyone says it there.'

If I was a really considerate host, I would have offered to relieve him of that hard package in his jeans – and maybe baked a cake.

'Night Nik, drive safely, keep your hands on the wheel,' I told him, and he laughed. 'Think unsexy thoughts like training early in cold water, or The Russian giving you a rub down.' Even that had me wincing at the thought.

He smiled and shook his head at me as I followed him to the door.

'I will see you tomorrow night for dinner, yeah? I'll book somewhere nice, pick you up at seven.' He didn't wait for an answer. 'Lock this door,' he said, as he opened it and moved into the hallway. I nodded and we held each other's gaze just long enough to make me super weak. He reached out and with his large hand, cupped one side of my face for just a moment, and then he smiled and walked away. I think I just melted to the spot.

'Lock the door,' he called back from the stairwell.

'Yes sir,' I snapped, closing and locking the door. I pressed my forehead against the door and breathed out. A man without a family who knows exactly what he wants and it is me – complicated men were definitely becoming my specialty.

Chapter 9

'Remember, no swearing Russian,' I said, glancing over to the 'wall' sitting next to me as we drove to Radio K-Talk where The Russian was to be a guest on the ten o'clock sports program.

'Fuck no, wouldn't dream of it,' he said, giving me a sly look. I returned his look with a touch of grimace and smartass. It takes some skill to do that, but I'm the girl for the job. The *Sports' Weekend Preview* program was on every Friday morning and I usually sent a player along. Some didn't need me to come with them; others like The Russian liked to have the media officer with him, made him feel important. He filled the front seat of my silver Alpha Spider convertible but refused to take his car – I think he also liked being chauffeured around by women.

'So Sasha, how's it going with you and the Kaiser, anything happening?' he asked.

'And I'd be telling you Russian because...?' I asked.

He grinned again. 'Because you like me.'

'Ha,' I scoffed. 'What gave you that idea?'

'I like that pantsuit you are wearing,' he said, glancing at my very groovy red pantsuit that I had just designed and made a prototype of before selling online. 'But I prefer you in a dress, you have good legs.'

I shook my head at him. 'Russian you must have breached a couple of discrimination acts in that last comment, you're a dinosaur. But thanks anyway. I prefer you in your soccer shorts but we'll both just have to put up with not seeing each other's legs.'

He was a good looking guy – strong, lean and chiseled. Nik was big but most of it was height; he was agile and fit, but The Russian was big everywhere that I could see.

'I'm a little disappointed you didn't ask me out, Sasha, instead of Kaiser,' he teased.

I glanced towards him and grinned. 'First, I didn't ask Kaiser out, and second, yeah, you and I would be a marriage made in heaven Russian,' I said with a laugh.

'Why? We get on,' he pushed. I knew he was teasing me and wouldn't touch me with a ten-foot pole, he was such a stirrer. I indicated to turn off the main road to the station.

'We would kill each other. Let's do a little test,' I said. 'Favorite program?'

'National Geographic,' he said. 'You?'

'Sports channel,' I told him. 'Favorite food?'

'Steak.'

'Eggplant lasagna,' I countered and he grimaced. 'Favorite music?'

'Rock.' The Russian scoffed as though it was everyone's choice.

'Jazz,' I said, 'favorite book?'

'Any sports magazine,' he said.

I held up my hand, 'I think I've proved my point. We would annoy the hell out of each other. What would we talk about?'

'Why would we have to talk?'

I tore my glance from the road long enough to give him another look.

'What? C'mon, everyone knows opposites attract. So what's the Kaiser got that I haven't?' he persisted.

'He speaks German,' I said.

The Russian nodded. 'Yeah, fair enough, that'd be high on my list too,' he teased.

I really wanted to ask The Russian what he knew about Nik but I didn't want to be seen to be checking up on him. He'd tell me when he's good and ready... wouldn't be soon enough. The best thing about The Russian though, is that he loved a bit of gossip and freely volunteered it.

'The girls love Nik you know, I've heard good reports that he's great in the sack,' he said.

I grimaced. 'Did I ask for a horizontal report card?'

'You know he got five offers from different clubs, and he came here.'

'I heard it was six. Maybe he likes the beach,' I offered.

'Maybe he wanted to get as far away from Berlin as possible. Some skeletons in the closet?'

'You telling or asking?' I said.

'Just saying he's a closed book. Captain couldn't get much from him either.'

'Mm, interesting. Nik and Lucas used to hang out a bit, so if he can't crack him, then maybe he doesn't want to be cracked,' I said. 'What do they say about you out there?'

The Russian shrugged. 'It'd be all good.'

'For sure,' I agreed, smiling to myself. I turned into the radio station parking lot and parked my car. We headed to reception and one of the journalists at the station – Dan who I went to college with – came out to greet us.

'Sasha, Russian, thanks for coming in, come this way.'

I followed Dan into the studio and he took The Russian into the booth. I sat outside with the producer until Dan's return.

'You didn't have to come,' Dan said, rejoining me.

'Tell Russian that. He likes to have his hand held.' I smiled at our Saints' soccer star through the glass separating the studio and he smiled back, the big ham.

'Hey, will you be at the game this Sunday?' Dan asked me.

'Yep, game day and I work for the Saints,' I said, summarizing it.

'Of course. I was thinking we should catch up sometime,' he said.

I looked at Dan and frowned. 'Yeah, well I'll see you at the game on Sunday.'

'Oh sure,' he said.

What the…? Seems it never rains but it pours guys. When you start seeing someone you suddenly become much more attractive to other guys for some weird reason. You must give off a pheromone that says *I'm attractive to a man therefore*

I'm attractive to all men. But seriously, Dan now? I busied myself tweeting to Saints' fans that The Russian was going to be on air in a few minutes. Then, the red light came on and The Russian came on live. I returned my concentration to the studio where he kept glancing out at me – the man loved an audience. I hope the announcer had his finger on the seven-second silence button because I doubted The Russian could go a whole conversation without dropping in a good swear word or two. I gave him the thumbs up after a well-thought-out answer.

I loved my job; here I was in a radio studio getting paid to keep an eye on The Russian and this Sunday was game day. Hell yeah, bring it on.

Chapter 10

I turned around in the mirror and looked at my outfit from all angles. Since Nick was taking me to a French restaurant, I decided to wear a French-inspired dress. A design somewhere between Coco Chanel's little black dress and the black Givenchy dress Audrey Hepburn wore in *Breakfast at Tiffany's* did the trick – I love a classic. I whipped it up and wore it fitted, just above the knee with a small sleeve. A small Oroton handbag, black court shoes and a string of cream pearls finished it off. I guess I was ready but I felt sick with nerves, and my stomach was somersaulting.

Nik was due any minute – okay fine, he had won, but I really wanted to go out for a good meal, that's it, no expectations or anything heavy. I hadn't been to *Lanterne* restaurant before, it was Nik's pick. And then I heard the knock at the door. Breathe, I told myself, and move towards the door and answer it.

Right I can do this.

I opened the door and my eyes grew huge; he was divine.

He looked good enough to eat in a light wool blend, two-piece gray suit with a single-breasted jacket and flat-front trousers. He completed the look with a crisp white shirt, open at the neck, no tie and polished black leather lace-ups. Clearly the suit I was repairing for him wasn't his only one. He smelled absolutely divine. He stepped in and before he could kiss me, I touched his jacket.

'Is that a Hugo Boss suit?' I asked, circling him and looking at the cut as he walked further into the room.

'Hi Sah-sha.' His lips curled into a smile.

'Oh, hi Nik.'

He laughed, leaned towards me and kissed me hello. Give up, really, resistance was futile, I was a goner. Crap.

'I think so.' He shrugged.

'What?' I said, losing all rational thought.

'I think it is a Hugo Boss,' he said. 'I had to wear it for a photoshoot, for a sponsor. I really liked it so I just got my manager to buy it.'

Really, he thinks it's a Boss?

That suit cost more than I earned in three months. It was made for Nik, just perfect. Yep such is the life of a mega-sports star, I think I'll just get my manager to whip out and buy some of my favorite designer labels, sigh! Why wasn't I good at sport? I wasn't bad at gymnastics but I couldn't earn a living from it.

He took my hand and twirled me under his arm in a smooth dance move.

'You look beautiful, Sah-sha,' he said, softly, 'just beautiful.'

I smiled. 'It's just something I had…' I never knew what

to say to compliments like that. I'm hoping that covered it.

He pulled me closer and looking straight into my eyes, he tried his compliment on me again.

'Sah-sha, you look beautiful.'

'Thank you,' I said, and he nodded with a smile.

'Shall we go?' he asked.

'Yes, see you soon Prada,' I told my pussycat and I grabbed my bag. This was the first time we were going to go in his car together, the first time we would walk into a restaurant together, the first official date. I locked up and we took the stairs to the street. He opened the car door for me and then came around and slid in beside me. There's something super sexy about sitting next to man in charge, watching him drive, his hands on the wheel, his command of everything. I particularly loved a sports watch on a man… don't know what that is about but it turns me on no end. I think I just orgasmed.

'Have you been to *Lanterne* before?' he asked.

'No. You?'

He shook his head. 'Your pick next time, Sah-sha,' he said.

There was going to be a next time? That was optimistic; we had to get through tonight first.

'I have a list of numbers should we need them tonight,' I said, 'the doctor, physical therapist, ambulance… and I can do the Heimlich maneuver.'

Nik put his head back and laughed, so fucking handsome.

'Any chance we're the same blood types?' he asked. 'I'm B-negative.'

I rolled my eyes. 'Of course you would be something special. Luckily I'm an O-type and everyone can have O-type.'

'Well we'll be right then,' Nik said. 'How did The Russian go on radio today?'

I told him as we drove along. I made a note to make sure our conversation tonight didn't center completely around the Saints, even though we didn't have much else in common – yet. Eventually we turned into the restaurant parking lot. He parked, leaped out and came around to open my door. He offered me his hand, helped me out of the car and took my hand as we walked along the boardwalk to the entrance.

We didn't get far before he was recognized and several fans asked for autographs and photos. I nodded for Nik to do it and he obliged them. He took my hand again and I saw the snap of flashes. It looked like we were going to be in the social pics.

A look of annoyance crossed his face. 'I'm sorry,' he said shielding me and opening the restaurant door. We huddled in.

'It's okay,' I said, and I gave him a small smile. I wasn't big on my life being out there, that's why I'm a journalist; I ask the questions not the other way around. But I didn't want Nik to see that, I could feel edginess coming off him in waves.

The maître d' greeted us at the door and apologized for the fuss outside. I don't know how they knew Nik would be there. Maybe he should have booked under an alias.

The maître d' showed us to a table in the corner. It had a view of the restaurant but could not be seen from the windows. Nik saw me into my seat then sat down opposite. I could see people in the restaurant checking us out and then I forgot them as his legs entwined around mine under the table. Nik took a deep breath.

'Are you okay?' I asked.

'I shouldn't have booked in my name, sorry. I forget sometimes… it's surreal… the publicity and…' His voice trailed off.

'Really, it's no big deal,' I assured him.

Then he got to the crux of it. 'I know you don't like that. I don't want you to be uncomfortable. We can make this work…'

I took his hand. 'Nik, really, I'm not worried, it's all good.' Wow, I must have given him the impression I'm a real flight risk.

He frowned as he read my face then nodded. We sat in silence as the waiter brought us water and two menus.

'Will you have champagne?' Nik asked me.

'In a French restaurant; of course,' I said. 'You order please.'

Nik smiled and glanced at the wine list. He gave the waiter an order and I found it on my list. Holy fuck, I truly can't afford to eat or drink here. Well I could, but I'd rather spend three hundred dollars on fabric than a meal for one. Nik must have read my expression because he lowered the menu and his voice.

'Sah-sha, I know you are independent and have your own career and life, but you must allow me to pay tonight, ja?' he said.

I frowned and opened my mouth to protest.

'No. I've invited you to dinner. You are my guest, I'm paying, I'm always paying even when you invite me to dinner,' he whispered. 'And there is no obligation, no payback, nothing. I just want your company.'

'As much as I'd like to live off you Nik and eat you broke, it hardly seems fair,' I said.

Nik grinned. 'You have invested time making yourself look beautiful tonight, let me repay the favor. Are we in agreeance?'

I really struggled with this; I didn't want to be bought and I didn't want to take advantage of him even though I know the cost of this meal was a drop in the ocean for him.

'Please Sah-sha, it's a simple request that would give me pleasure,' he said.

I nodded. 'Thank you, Nik, I accept.'

He smiled as though he had won the lottery, funny guy.

'So…' I lifted my menu, 'do you know what's good?'

'Yes I do, and I think we should order very different dishes so we can share. Do you share?' he asked.

'Oh I share,' I said, and he smiled again.

I wished I could have sex with him right now, get it out of my system and then I could concentrate on eating. I'd have a bigger appetite then. He shuffled in his seat. I wonder if Nik was thinking the same thing. What the heck, I'm direct, let's put it out there. I closed my menu and leaned towards him.

'It's very hard to concentrate on food when all I can think about is your naked body on top of mine,' I said.

Nik's mouth fell open and he shut it abruptly and swallowed.

I continued, 'I wish we could do it right now on this table, just fuck each other silly, then have a really nice glass of champagne afterward and dine. I'm always hungry after sex,' I told him.

He made this growling sound in his throat and slowly shut the menu. He lowered his voice to match mine.

'Sah-sha, what am I supposed to do with that?' He exhaled.

I grinned and opened my menu. 'Just saying,' I told him.

With one finger, he pulled the menu down that I held in front of me.

'You are wicked, Sah-sha, wicked.' He sat back looking much more uncomfortable in his chair. Lucky the tablecloths were really long.

The waiter appeared with the champagne, showed Nik the label and skillfully popped it open, and poured two glasses. Nik's eyes returned to me, never leaving my face, his breathing slightly jagged. I smiled at him, thanked the waiter and raised a glass.

'To good health,' I said, offering my favorite toast.

Nik picked up his glass. 'To beauty,' he said, and clinked it against mine.

The champagne was delicious: dry, cold and bubbly. Nik cleared his throat and returned to the menu looking most uncomfortable.

'So how do you know what is good if you haven't been here?' I asked.

'I asked my manager. He did his research and told me.'

'Really, he gets paid for that?'

'He didn't mind bringing his wife here a few times and trying it out. He calls it a bonus.' Nik shrugged. 'So,' he glanced down the menu, 'he suggests… oh fuck it, I can't think now.'

I gave him a smile and he shook his head and smiled darkly at me. He threw the menu down.

'I'm ruined,' he declared.

*****

Eventually we managed to order and it was good, so good. Nik's phone pinged a few times during the meal, he apologized and put it on silent. I was so impressed. I wondered who it was… some girl?

After coffee, I went to the ladies and he paid while I was away. I love that too. Some paparazzi awaited us as we came out and again he rushed me to the car and saw me in, returning to his side.

'Why do they do that?' he asked, 'who cares that we're dining out?'

'People love gossip,' I said, with a shrug. 'Just ask The Russian.'

'Yeah, he loves the inside scoop. He's been pumping me since I got here,' Nik agreed.

'Thank you, for dinner, for tonight, it was wonderful,' I said sincerely to him.

'The pleasure is mine. Didn't I tell you it would be great, Süsse?' Nik started the car and pulled out of the parking lot. As we drove, he reached across and held my hand; good thing it was an automatic car.

I felt such a heady rush; I wish it could always be like this. I know love deepened and the relationship developed if it was meant to, but there was nothing like first date excitement.

'What are you up to tomorrow?' he asked.

'I'm doing gym in the morning, then Max and I are going to a fashion designer exhibition and I'm doing Saffron's wedding dress tomorrow night. She's coming around for another fitting,' I said. I didn't want to move too fast or be on tap for Nik; there were plenty of girls on hand to do that.

'Any catwalk flips?' he teased, with a glance towards me.

'I'll probably fit four or five in. And you?' I asked.

'No, and no handstands, but I'm training in the morning, then Lucas invited me around to watch the game, and I need to get some clothes soon, but I can't face it,' he said. 'Will you shop with me?'

'Hell yeah,' I said, way too enthusiastically, 'but we can't do it now until next spare weekend.'

'I can wait,' he said.

'Alice said you had only one suitcase of clothes with you when you moved in. Seriously, is that it?' I asked.

Nik nodded. 'I'll need to speak with Alice, she's infiltrating my spy ring and giving away secrets.'

I laughed. This man was so gorgeous and I was going to shop with him!

'So you are too busy for me tomorrow,' he said, sadly.

'You can't talk,' I ribbed him. 'You're spending the afternoon with Lucas.'

'I'd drop Lucas in a heartbeat Sah-sha, to spend time with you. Besides, last few times we've traveled, Lucas and I have had to share a room – we get plenty of bonding time,' he teased. 'He spends a long time in the bathroom.'

'Mm, that's good information to store,' I said.

'I didn't tell you that,' Nik said.

I wished the drive home was longer. We were almost there. I can't believe I was saying that – I'm such a yo-yo.

'What time will you get to the game on Sunday?' he asked.

'I help in the VIP membership area from about ten and then I head to the media box before eleven. The journos don't get in too early. What about you?'

'Ah… eleven-thirty start, so I'll be there after nine or so to get strapped and psyched. Are you going to the *Shaken Not Stirred* bar afterward?' he asked. Nik was getting his weekend sorted.

'Nope, I never do.'

'Why?' he asked, glancing towards me. 'I thought you'd be a party girl.'

I shook my head. 'I don't go where the players go. I leave that to the groupies and girlfriends. Some of my friends and I go to the *Ska Bar*.'

'I like ska music! But I don't know that place,' he said. 'I have to see you Sunday.'

'Then let's lock it in,' I agreed, and he visibly relaxed. This man was going to be the end of me. What a way to go. He pulled into my apartment block.

'Would you like to come up?' I asked.

'Yes,' he said and turned off the ignition.

We were a very direct pair. He held my hand as we took the stairs, and my body was betraying me already; I was excited and nervous, the butterflies in my stomach were unbelievable. You would think I had never done this before!

And then Nik blew it.

'Those phone numbers weren't needed after all Sah-sha,' he said, 'we lived to tell.'

He jinxed it. Sitting on my doorstep was Saffron. The wedding was off. Fuck on so many levels.

Chapter 11

Nik was so understanding – he brushed my cheek, kissed me and left me to take care of Saffron with her swollen face from crying. I watched his gorgeous butt descending the stairs, my body ached for him but my heart was breaking for Saffy – catastrophe! I unlocked the door and led my twin sister to the sofa and went to make us both a cup of tea. I knew all about relationship pain, but I also knew not to run down her fiancé, Daniel; he was a really nice guy and this might be fixable.

Minutes later, I put her cup of tea in front of her and sat next to Saffy on my white sofa. Prada bolted, the scaredy-cat; he wasn't good with crying women.

'Saffy, take a deep breath, a mouthful of tea, and if you feel up to it, tell me what happened,' I said 'If not, I can put you straight to bed. The guest room is made up.'

She nodded and followed instructions. Wow, I was on a roll lately… I must try it on The Russian, and see if he obeys.

Saffy took a deep breath, wiped her eyes and took a sip of tea. I hated seeing my twin so distraught especially when Saffron was such a sweet, up-person. The only times I remember her crying were when our family dog Muffy died – we all cried then – and when our brothers had a food fight with our birthday cake. Daniel was really her first big love. I was hoping she'd cruise through life unhurt.

'Sassy, Dan said he's not sure he's ready to be married,' she said, choking on the words.

Oh not good, so not good.

'Okay, let's break this down,' I said to her. 'He still wants to be with you?'

She nodded. 'He said he does, but he wants to do more things before settling down. He's got cold feet.'

'What things did he say, exactly?' I asked.

'He said we should delay the wedding and do some travel, work overseas, maybe see more of our friends – and we both know what that means, he wants to meet other women. He's not sure.' She started crying again, heart-wrenching sobs, each one like a cut in my chest.

'Saffy, we don't know that, stop, listen,' I said. 'Remember when you graduated from teachers' college and you wanted to go abroad for a year?'

She nodded, picking up her tea and cupping it in her hands.

'Remember Daniel didn't want to go? He wanted to get a few years' work experience under his belt first and then do a working holiday. You were worried being married to him might be like wearing 'cement boots' – your words. You were worried that he might tie you down. Remember?' I challenged her.

'Yes.' She stopped crying long enough to look at me and take my words in.

'You had plans to do big things then, but you adapted and let him get his work experience under the belt. You both forgot that dream of traveling and went straight to the marriage step. What if… and I'm just guessing here, what if you bring the travel and working overseas dream back again – it was your idea first, not Daniel's. Delay the wedding until you've had some more adventure. Hell, if you're going to be together for life, what's a few years?' I said.

She stopped crying while she thought. 'I had forgotten about that.'

'But Saffy, I'm no expert at this, remember I had an impulse marriage that didn't work,' I said. 'I'm just saying it's not a big deal that he wants to delay the wedding, he still wants you, right?'

'Yes, he said that over and over.'

'You've compromised for him before, but now he's kind of reminding you of your original dream,' I said.

'Why can't we get married and then travel, like on our honeymoon?' she asked.

'Maybe he wants to use a bit of the wedding money to travel before you blow it all on the big day and then have to start paying off a mortgage,' I suggested. 'So, do it in reverse, let him propose in every romantic spot you visit, or you do the same. Have the honeymoon first and the wedding later… just a thought. Maybe he's looking at our parents or his folks and thinking marriage means settling down and being sensible, when all he wants is to be with you and have fun.' That was good, I surprised myself.

She nodded. 'You might be right Sassy. I might have overreacted, kind of panicked, you know? I need to go and talk with him.' She rose and I got up with her.

'Want me to drive you?' I only had two champagnes a couple of hours ago and was up to the task.

'No, I've got my car here, thanks.'

I walked her to the door and she hugged me.

'Thanks for helping me see sense,' Saffron said and pulled away. 'I'm sorry I ruined your date.'

I shrugged. 'You didn't, I'll see Nik again on Sunday. But you and Daniel, you love each other, you'll sort it out.'

She smiled and opened the door, grabbing her keys and jacket from the side table. 'I love you Sassy.'

'I love you, Saffy,' I said, and watched her head down the stairs. I closed and locked the door. Problem temporarily solved and Nik gone home to bed. Damn. I was never going to get to bed with Nik, at this rate, I'd have to get a vibrator. I wondered if German vibrators were any different.

*****

I sent a message to Saffron as soon as I woke the next morning and she replied back to report that all was good with her and Daniel and that she would call me later. Thank you saints in heaven for that, but I guess she wouldn't be needing the dress in any hurry.

Ah, Saturday… all day, yes! I didn't message Nik because

I knew he'd be at training, but I would call him later to thank him for dinner and see if he thought of me last night, if he could sleep because I couldn't. I wondered if he'd tell me if I asked? Probably, as he's so direct. Mm, forget the vibrator – picturing Nik in the shower or lying in bed worked for me.

I did my gym workout and finished with my sit-ups, all fueled with sexy thoughts of Nik; doesn't hurt to fantasize. Despite all my efforts at resisting him, if I didn't have Nik soon I was going to implode and it wouldn't be pretty. Bits of me all over the place – tragic. I showered and changed into a pinafore with a long-sleeved shirt underneath, tights and boots. Today, I had plans and ninety minutes later, Max and I were swanning around the display stands at the Designer and Bridal Expo.

We worked together sometimes, slipping each other business where we could – as well as hairdressing Max did bridal makeup and the bridal market was a growing part of his business. Bridal dresses were a growing part of mine too, but I didn't really want to make dresses, I wanted to design them; you know custom make and design for the bride. I had my own designs on my website and I liked to look at the bride's figure and design what would accentuate her assets and hide those that she wasn't as fond of featuring.

'These sites look like crap,' Max whispered in my ear as we passed a few ordinary looking stands. He was such a bitch sometimes.

'Here we are,' I said, and we stopped in front of the display where our businesses were on show. We didn't want a stand of our own – too expensive and we were small fry in this game, but on the group stand we were given a small area to display our photos and cards.

'Looks good,' I said, eyeing off Max's beautiful bridal hair and makeup photos with his business cards propped next to them. Beside his display were my illustrations of my bridal designs and a rack of my business cards. We played it cool as a couple of gals came over and hovered near our display. They were making a day of it with their sample bags in tow. I grabbed one of Max's cards and so they could overhear, I started gushing to him.

'This guy did my sister's hair and make-up; it was fantastic. I'm going to use him too,' I said, with a wink to Max and waved around his business card.

The girls reached for Max's card and put it in their sample bags. We wandered off and left them looking at the photos.

'I owe you a coffee for that Sash,' Max said.

'Only if the business comes through, Maxie. Let's get a seat.' We headed to the catwalk area where seats were filling fast. The next bridal parade was due to start in fifteen minutes. Next year I hoped to have a few of my own designs in the parades. We sat and I watched as Max ran a hand through his perfectly coiffured, sandy-colored hair. Everything about him said neat. I always felt a bit messy sitting next to him, like a whirlwind had ruffled me up but just missed him.

'It looks good,' I teased him.

'Mm, too blond.' He shook his head. I grinned and squeezed his arm as the music began to swell. I loved a good parade and then just to take the sparkle out of my day, I saw my ex, Adam – he was wearing a work pass around his neck – damn and the day was going so well. I sank a little lower in my seat and watched him; he was always as sexy as hell when he was working. The way he moved, the way he angled himself and the camera, and more fool me for thinking I'm special because so did the model on the catwalk that he was shooting. So special that he gave her a wink and she gave him a special smile. Sigh, thank God he's my ex-husband. Max is right; it was a good thing he was out of my life.

Chapter 12

Game day! It was a beautiful day, clear and bright and we were going to beat the Houston Harriers. Right, got that sorted, now to the game. I wasn't tired despite not sleeping well – it was the result of a good cause after all.I had visions of Nik kissing me, those blue eyes staring into mine, his shirt coming off and my hands running over that washboard stomach and all his other parts. I might never sleep again.

You would think I would learn to be just a little cautious after one failed marriage that was born from being impetuous in love. It appears I didn't get that cautious gene. And first thing this morning, I got a message from Nik to say he couldn't wait to see me at the game. I told him all the things I couldn't wait to see about him – it was a long text. I can't believe I feel this great, scary, scary stuff.

When I got to the ground, the Houston Harrier buses were already arriving, their fans decked out in burgundy and white. I knew Nik would be in the change rooms preparing, and I spotted his VW in the players' parking lot – that gave me a little chill, knowing we were so close. I swung mine into the staff allocation. I thought about him getting strapped and iced, hmm.

I whipped up to the media room to check all was okay; later I would stay there to watch the game with the other journos. I had to do updates on our social media pages throughout the game with the key points like goals, penalties, injuries and any great action. I didn't need to put out a release after the game because the media present had that covered and it went onto the national media wires.

It was a bit of a fine line for Alice and me as she usually looked after the social media, but only in a social sense while I did the news angle. Tomorrow she would put up great photos from the game for the supporters. The radio networks especially followed my updates because they were timely.

All was well in the media room and I headed off to the VIP marquee to see if Kay or Jim needed any help.

'Hey Sash.' I heard a voice and turned to see Alice leading the Saints' mascot to the children's area. 'Thanks for saving you know who,' she grinned, 'he's one very happy Saint.'

I smiled back. 'The things I do for this club,' I teased and with a wave, promised to catch her later. I kept going. On the way to the VIP area I passed by Shayne and a couple of the opposition management team. He gave me the thumbs up and kept going. I stuck my head into the VIP marquee area where a champagne brunch was being served to those guests who paid to be members and enjoy the benefits including VIP seating. Jim was on the microphone calling up some unsuspecting person to draw their raffle.

'All okay?' I asked, sidling up to Kay and squatting down beside her as she sat at the staff table.

'We're under control, thanks for checking in though,' she said. 'Um…' she looked over my shoulder and smiled. 'I think someone is trying to get your attention.'

I turned to see Nik standing to the side of the entrance to the marquee, hiding as much as possible and beckoning me out. He was in the team's training gear and looked wonderfully kissable. Unfortunately my boss Jim saw him at the same time.

'Ladies and gentlemen; don't say we don't look after you here, look who has just dropped in.' He pointed the audience to the entrance where Nik's eyes widened in surprise.

The VIP members turned to look at the entrance like a pack watching a tennis game and on seeing Nik, gave him a huge cheer and burst into applause. He froze like a deer in the headlights, gave an embarrassed sort of wave and began to back out with a quick chin up motion to me to follow him.

Jim was walking towards him. 'C'mon Nik, not so fast, just a few questions for our loyal supporters and then we'll let you go.'

Nik gave me a look that said rescue me and I smiled with sympathy and shrugged. Jim was my boss after all and he had Nik by the arm, even if he only came up to Nik's armpit. The audience was still applauding.

'Now as you know,' Jim was saying, 'Niklas Wagner or the Kaiser as the boys call him, joined us this season from

Germany and we're pretty happy to have him. So where's home Nik?' Jim asked pushing the microphone in Nik's face.

'Um, Berlin, but I'm really loving it here, especially the beach,' Nik said, winning the audience over.

A hand shot up in the audience which just happened to be attached to the arm of a very attractive woman in her mid-thirties or so. She looked as though she had just stepped off the set of *The Housewives of Santa Ana*.

'Ah, we have a question,' Jim said, nodding to the woman. 'Just one because I know you've got to go and get ready for the game and we don't want the coach down here looking for you.'

The woman stood up. 'I was just going to offer Nik a home-cooked meal if he got homesick. I make a very good Apple Strudel from an old German recipe,' she said. The audience burst out laughing, Nik grinned good-naturedly – it wouldn't be the first offer he had – and he gave her a wave of thanks. He nodded to Jim and bolted for the door. Damn, should I be able to cook strudel? Note to self, check recipe.

'A round of applause for Nik, good luck today,' Jim was saying, as Nik made a hasty exit, diverting by me to grab my hand in retreat. I followed him out, laughing. I could hear Jim still carrying on about what a great game they were expecting from our new German recruit and how he had been a great asset to the team this season already.

Nik pulled me around the corner of the marquee, looked around and then stopped to look at me. He smiled. 'Hello gorgeous Sah-sha, next time I'm going to phone you from outside to come out and meet me.'

'Hello Nik,' I said, and looked up at him with way too

much excitement in my face, God I'm a pushover. 'What are you doing here?' I asked, rubbing my hands up his arms.

'Ah you need to stop that,' he said, and leaned in to kiss me. I think the relief ebbed through us both at the touch of our lips, like we could get through the day now. 'No really, you need to stop it.' I looked down and realized the track pants didn't hide much. I giggled like a naughty schoolgirl.

'Thank you for being so understanding last night,' I said, touching his face.

'Is Saffron all right?' he asked.

'I think she and Daniel will be fine,' I said. His eyes watched me all the time, watched my lips as I talked, rose to my eyes, my eyelashes, back to my lips. This man was hellishly sexy.

'I didn't sleep at all last night, you kept me awake,' he said, still holding me in his arms.

I loved that he was so upfront and just said things like that – not worried if it was too much to put out there or it made him vulnerable. God, this was freaking me out – how good I felt. I kind of thought after Adam that maybe I'd had a great love and that was it, now all the feelings were so raw and real, a second chance at love.

'You kept me awake all night too,' I said, 'You'll be busy on the ground, but I hope it's a good game or else I'm bound to fall asleep in the middle of my reporting duties.'

He grinned. 'Sah-sha, it will be a great game, power of positive thought… we are going to go out there and get them!' He stopped. 'Sorry we just had our pep talk from the coach,' he said with a sheepish grin. 'We didn't make plans for tonight. I will go and have a few drinks with the boys and then I can meet you if you like?'

'That would be great. I'll go to the *Ska Bar* but you don't have to come there, we can go to my place if you don't want to party on.'

'I'll get there and then we can go to your place later, ja, I mean yes?' he translated.

'Yah,' I teased him, well it sounded like that anyway. He gave me a satisfied grin as though he had everything worked out now. He took a deep breath and pulled away.

'I've got to go before Lucas realizes I'm missing and kicks my butt. Walk me back?'

'Sure.' We walked through the grounds towards the players' rooms when I heard a wolf whistle. I turn around to see Dan, the journo from the local radio station; I gave him a wave.

Nik glared past me. 'Who was that?'

'Dan's just an old friend, he's a sport reporter for K-Talk, and he produces the sports show that Russian crashed on Friday.'

'Does he like you?' Nik asked, his eyes narrowed as he continued to glare in the direction of Dan.

'Of course, I'm likable,' I said, declaring the obvious.

Nik rolled his eyes as he turned to face me, his lips were a thin line. 'I know that Sah-sha, but that's not what I mean. Is he – '

I cut him off. 'I'm not interested in him.' I grabbed his jaw. 'Unlock your jaw.'

He swallowed. 'It's not locked.'

'Your jaw is locked and your eyes are narrow,' I said, releasing his chin from my grasp.

'Does he sit in the media box with you?' Nik asked.

'Every game, all last year too. I've known him a long time. I'm not interested,' I said, keeping it as black and white as I could. My ex-husband had played horrendous jealousy games with me and I wasn't going there again and I wouldn't inflict that on anyone.

He made a guttural sound in his throat. I leaned up and kissed him and his jaw relaxed; he looked down at me and softened. He walked with his arm around my shoulder, while I was nicely tucked next to him. I loved that he was tall and muscled but not a wall like The Russian. Nik was fit and agile.

We came around a corner and got sprung. Someone called out his name and before we knew it, he was mobbed by fans that had got to the grounds early to spot the players. I looked around and beckoned for one of the security guys to come over and help clear the way to the rooms. It's part of the marketing team's job – it's better if we or security move the players along, than have the players tell the fans they can't stick around. He signed autographs as he continued to weave towards the gate. We got separated and I saw him look back when he got to the change rooms and look for me. He found me for a second, gave me a smile and disappeared.

I was in so much lust and like, and maybe love, who knows but I hadn't fallen in this deep for a long time. *Come on in* my heart was telling me, the water was just fine.

*****

I got my laptop set up in the media room; I loved working from there, such a great view of the game. The room was filling up and I chatted to the usual journos as we waited for the game to start. Drinks and sandwiches were delivered and everyone helped themselves. I grabbed two Diet Colas… not that many of the journos wanted low-calorie, just me and Carly – one of the ladies from *The Sports Daily* – and I took one over to her. She was a tall, slim girl – a professional basketballer who also reported at sporting games.

'Thanks Sash,' she took it and opened it right away. 'Was that the Kaiser I saw you cozying up to before? That new?'

'Pretty new,' I said, taking a gulp of my drink. She reached for a couple of sandwiches.

'I could have sworn you told me that you'd rather masturbate than go out with a player when you worked around them all day,' she teased me.

'Yeah, well my fingers got sore,' I shot back and she laughed.

'Lucky you,' she said, and squeezed my arm. 'What about that Russian? I met him at the press conference the other day, he's big – a very good size for me. Is he single?'

'He's a wall,' I agreed. 'Newly single.'

She groaned. 'Not touching that.'

'I'll let him know that if he needs a date for the Best and Fairest Awards though, that you'll play handbag?' I asked.

'Hell yeah, that I could do, and he'd actually be taller than me which would be nice for a change,' she said, 'I could wear heels.'

I grinned and headed back to my chair next to Dan and

within minutes the game began with the teams running on the field. My stomach always fluttered with nerves; I can only imagine how the players felt with all that pressure on them. It was even more intense now that Nik was in my orbit.

The Houston Harriers came on first, did a lap and got a good response. They were a good side, third on the ladder so far, we were second so it was going to be a competitive game. Then the Santa Ana Saints came on, led by Captain Lucas – he stopped and gave each player a pep talk as they moved past him. I loved watching the boys come out to play; The Russian was all fired up, well as much as he could be given he didn't do anything with any great pace; Ed was doing short, sharp runs, back and forward and sideways; Tomás was jittery but that was part of his job as goalkeeper; and my Nik looked calm and superb. I saw his eyes sweep over the other side of the ground, assessing the Harriers, then he had a few words to Lucas before jogging into central midfielder position. The siren went and I drew a breath as the game started.

I put my radio earphone bud in one ear so I could hear the radio live commentary which was set up in the next room, and kept my other ear free to hear any comments around me. The game was tight; neither team gave each other any ground and I had to keep tearing my eyes off Nik to make sure I watched all the guys. I posted randomly as play unfolded.

We held our breath as the ball went dangerously close to the goals but Tomás did one of his legendary dives and sent it packing. We held our breaths again in the media box when Lucas found the net after the second attempt following a mix up in our backline. Johan our coach would have a word to say about that when they analyzed the game during the week. *Defend, defend, defend and stick to your man!* I could hear him now.

Then my guy, yeah, I'm claiming him... Nik did an excellent strike from the edge of the box and brought it home for the team's first goal. I listened to the broadcast guys as they raved about it – 'Legendary!', 'That's what we're talking about', and 'They've paid an awful lot for this young man and I'd say it was well invested.'

Yep, damn fine investment, I'd say.

Chapter 13

I didn't want to be with other people tonight, I wanted to be with Nik. I thought about it a lot during the day; I'm not sure I could be as open with my feelings as Nik could – maybe if I had met him before Adam, but once bitten, twice shy; once burnt, twice singed, I think I made that last one up but you get the picture. Half a dozen of my friends were at the *Ska Bar*; I just wanted to taste Nik. I got his text a few hours after the game.

NIK: Done post-game drinks, want to escape. Need to see you

ME: Same. Where?

NIK: Your place, 20 mins?

ME: See you there. Can't wait

That was big for me. BIG. I had given Adam everything – all my faith and love, hope, trust, virginity, everything and in return I got hot sex, a hot guy and a shitload of drama. Now, I wanted to meet Nik halfway, but to be honest I was terrified. I spent a lot of time putting up all these walls to protect myself and they weren't going to come down overnight, but I was working on it. Even putting that little bit extra on my message took a deep breath and a lot of bravery. For Nik, it seemed so easy, probably nothing.

I said a quick goodbye to my friends and raced home. I wanted to get home before he arrived so I could shower and change into fresh clothes – get the club smell off me. I raced in, had a shower and changed into jeans and a loose off-the-shoulder gypsy top in white. I slipped on some white ballet slippers. I really should be sewing tonight; I had orders but the only order I wanted was the command to hit the sheets with Nik. Nothing, and I mean nothing, was going to stop me from having sex with him tonight… with luck.

He was right on time – German precision – I like that, and by the time I got to the door I was so nervous it was insane. I don't even get nervous presenting my media strategy to the board – I figure I know this stuff, they don't, who gives a fuck? But I could barely breathe when I opened the door to him. He waltzed in wearing jeans, a black button-down shirt and dress shoes; man this guy could dress himself. His eyes looked so blue and with his tan and blond hair, he was breathtaking. He didn't speak, just picked me up, kicked the door closed with his foot and kissed me.

It was one hell of a kiss. My feet still weren't on the ground as his tongue slipped between my lips and I sucked on it, making him groan. He was hard, all over, and eventually he pulled away and put me down.

He grinned at me. 'Hello, Sah-sha, hello Prada,' he looked around and greeted my cat. He returned his gaze to me. 'You look so beautiful,' he said, as he ran his hands along my bare shoulders and down my back. I suspect he noticed I had no bra on; it was an off-the-shoulder top, and I was at home after all.

My throat was so tight and my stomach was full of butterflies. I said the safest thing: 'You had a great game, congrats.'

'Thanks, it went well.' He shrugged casually.

I knew the kind of pressure he was under to perform. You didn't get contracts like his without a pile of expectations on your shoulders.

'No, you were brilliant today and right now, you look... delicious,' I said, still holding his arms and looking up at him.

'Good enough to eat?' he asked.

'Absolutely.'

'I haven't seen your bedroom yet,' he said with a glance to my suspended room. 'I've come close a few times,' he said, his lips curling up slightly into a smile.

'You can see it from here,' I teased him. It was open and on display – but there was only one way up there. 'Would you like a tour?' I asked.

'Yes, right now would be good,' he said.

My eyes flicked to the bulge in his jeans and back to the stairs to my room. Seems like there was no time like the present.

'Allow me.' I took his hand and undertook the job of tour leader. He was so close behind me I swear I couldn't have fitted a condom between us. When we got to the top of the stairs, he stopped and took in my suspended bedroom.

'This is great,' he said, removing his gaze from me for just a moment while he took in the room. 'Very you, Sah-sha.'

'Yeah? Thanks,' I said, studying the room again to work out exactly what that meant. The room was in alignment with the top triangle of the large windows and a row of trees outside the window – it was like being in a treehouse and totally private. The bed was in the center of the room and a large candle-like chandelier in white crystals hung from the middle of the room. The quilt and sheets were red and gold and I had stacks of pillows because I liked being piled high.

'Now I have seen your room Sah-sha,' he said as he turned to me, 'I want to see every inch of you.'

I choked on air and began spluttering. Nik laughed and reached for my hand, then led me to the bed.

'Lie with me for a while,' he said. He kicked off his shoes and I did the same. I'm guessing he was pretty exhausted after the intensity of the game. He sat on the edge of the bed, then leaned back on the pillows and pulled me next to him. I nestled against his chest – this was so nice, so relaxing, undemanding, and intimate.

I put my hand on his chest and felt him breathing. He still had an impressive bulge in his jeans that was keen to be released but he was taking it very slowly.

'This is the first time all day I have relaxed,' he said, 'so good to be here with you Sah-sha.' He said the words softly, near my ear and I drank them in. I needed this more than he would know, just to breathe him in and top up on Nik. To feel like nothing or no-one else mattered, for tonight at least. I knew he would make his move when he was ready but I knew he needed me to be okay with it as well. I hadn't really made it easy for him.

As he held me tightly against him, I ran my fingers over his chest, trailing up his arms, every now and then just passing by the top of his jeans, enough to put his body on alert. He winced as I touched near his rib and I leaned up and gently pulled up his shirt. He was black with bruises from the game.

'Ouch, that hurt?' I asked.

'Really badly,' he teased. 'You should kiss it better.'

'Think that will help?' I asked, looking at his blue eyes as they appraised me.

'If Doc was here, he'd prescribe it,' Nik insisted.

I grinned at him and slowly undid the buttons on his shirt, pulling it back to reveal his chest. It was a glorious sight that I'm sure I would never get sick of – lean, muscular, tanned with a spattering of bruises and some interesting ink that started on his side and continued to his back. I would have to explore that later. I leaned in and pressed my lips to his ribs. His body tensed and his hand ran through my hair.

'It's sore here too, Sarsh.' He abbreviated my name and pointed to the other side of his chest.

'Really? You poor thing.' I moved my lips to the other side of his chest at his direction.

'And here.' He pointed down lower. I flicked him a suspicious glance and he laughed. That sexy dimple appeared again near his chin and then he winced. 'Ouch, that did hurt. Don't make me laugh.'

I caught him by surprise, trailing my fingernails down

his jeans over his erection, and his breath hissed through his teeth. He said something in German but I think it was good. He put his hands under my arms and rolled me over, leaning over the top of me. He studied me as though he wanted to remember the moment, moving in to kiss me and then he moved down my neck and over my bare shoulders. Gentle, seductive kisses, all the time his strong arms holding his weight above me, his body flexing. He was so sexy and I kept forgetting to breathe, so I was constantly gasping for small pockets of air.

He began to lower my top, my heart rate when into turbo drive and then Nik made this hungry, groaning sound in his throat. His touch makes my body burn.

'Nik,' I said, my hand running through his longer locks to his short cropped, blond hair at the back and sides.

'Mm?' he said, not looking up. I couldn't speak and realizing I was frozen, he looked at me.

'Sah-sha?' he said, concern on his face.

'Don't stop,' I gasped.

He chuckled. 'Then don't interrupt me. I'm very busy.'

'But I want you naked,' I said, noticing we were both still dressed.

'Be patient,' he instructed me. 'I don't want to miss anything. Next time, we'll tear each other's clothes off, but tonight I have to get all these images in my mind to last me until I see you next.'

He lowered his gaze again. I'm glad he didn't look at me with the tears I tried to blink out of my eyes. I loved that he wanted to memorize my body and this moment, as though it was important to him.

'Beautiful,' he said, even though I was a bit colt-like and not like the woman he had bedded. I felt an urgent aching to have him, almost a dull pain... I hadn't felt that for a long while.

Please don't let me come yet, I begged the goddess of orgasms. I hadn't had sex for over a year, since filing for divorce I had lost my appetite for it, but this was good... I needed this. My back arched and I moaned with pleasure. Nik's hand moved down to my jeans, undoing them and he pulled away from my breasts long enough to pull them down. I helped, then struggled to get his off and he removed them swiftly.

'Slow down wildcat,' he said, with a smile. I tried to but I wanted to see him naked, I wanted to see every inch of him but Nik wasn't in for quick ride; he was in for an experience.

'These are cute, Sah-sha,' he said holding my hips down and admiring my white lace boy panties. He ran a finger around the edges and I shuddered from the charge between us; I think he gave me an electric shock again.

'I want to see you,' I complained, wiggling away from him and forcing him onto his side. He sighed and I pushed him a bit further to get him onto his back.

'So bossy, Sarsh,' he teased me and obliged.

'Oh wow,' I said, making him laugh again. I gazed at his body – a super-hot, amazing sight, I wished I could take a photo.

'You've seen one before haven't you?' he asked, with a raised eyebrow.

'Not like this,' I flattered him, wrinkling my nose at him.

I sat on my haunches, topless and only wearing my lace panties, and worked my way between his legs.

'What are you doing?' he asked, amused, watching me. 'You know I was in the middle of something – you, actually.'

'I want to memorize your body and this night too,' I said, 'such a good idea.' I wedged myself between his long, powerful, tanned legs, and admired his body. Glorious.

'Can I get back to you now?' he asked, leaning up on his elbows.

'Shh, no,' I said. I just wanted to touch him. I don't know why the urge overtook me, but he looked so powerful and smelled so good. He reached for me again and I stopped him.

'Nik, don't make me come up there,' I threatened him. 'My room, my rules.'

He smiled, and then groaned.

I trailed my nails gently over him; I looked up at his chest and that's when I noticed them again – small scars, round and a mixture of gashes; most hidden by ink. And then Nik's eyes narrowed as he saw me looking. I ran my hand up to circle one of the scars and he grabbed my hand and pulled it away from his body.

'Wait, Sarsh,' he said, and took charge. He sat up, hurriedly pushed me back on the bed and brought himself down on me.

'Those scars...' I said.

'Nothing. Just from years of sport,' he said. I studied his face and he gave nothing away, it was locked, devoid of all emotion. Then he licked his lower lip, his eyes questioning mine; I couldn't imagine him looking more uncomfortable. I lay on my back looking up at him and I grabbed his jaw.

'You're doing that lock jaw thing again,' I said, looking into his eyes. 'What's wrong? Are you okay?'

He nodded.

'Nik?'

'Just let me have you, Sah-sha,' he said, 'I've been getting off on this for days, but now you are really here.' He dropped my gaze and returned his eyes to my body. He exhaled, as though he was refocusing. He was pressing into me and he hadn't lost interest. Just when I thought he was about to go inside me, he pushed himself down the bed and held down my hips with his large hands. My stomach clenched and I dropped my head back on the bed. Nik felt me tense.

'It's okay, Sah-sha, I won't hurt you,' he said.

'I know,' I answered.

'Do you? I want this to be good for you... special,' he said.

I didn't have any words to offer; I had heard a promise like that once before, even if I still needed to hear it again.

'But you don't know that of course,' he said in the softest voice. 'You have to learn to trust me and maybe to like me, and then to love me.'

Please Nik, please stop talking – the words were too much. His strong hands made me feel secure but my breathing was erratic and my heart beat was racing. This was it… my uncomplicated life was no more, I was in – heart and soul. He began performing his magic, this time off the field.

'For the love of God,' I groaned with pleasure. The heat from his mouth on my body trailed all the way through me, touching every inch of me. I wanted this more than anything but waves of vulnerability pushed over me fighting the feelings of need.

'Nik,' I called his name, I needed to hear his voice.

'I have you, Sah-sha,' he answered, 'I have you.'

And he did, he worked me. For the love of God, no wonder the girls said he was sensitive. My mind was tripping on his words; my body was tripping on his touch. I wanted them separate so I could think about them and go over them a million times, but it was a rush of all my senses.

Slowly, he worked on me. I couldn't take my eyes off the ceiling because my back was so arched in pleasure. He increased the pace and the heat. I cried out needing this, wanting this more than I knew. The muscles in my body tightened. So intense. I cried out and came like I've never experienced before and then I dropped back on the bed and I felt his soft breath, tingling me before he moved up and pulled me against his chest.

'I'm speechless,' I stuttered.

Nik gave me a satisfied grin. 'Really? I wouldn't have thought that was possible.' He looked at me as though my statement was fiction. I would have smacked him on the arm but I couldn't raise my hand.

He ran his eyes over me and returned them to hold my gaze, studying me with such intensity. A smile traced his lips and he slowly lowered his lips to mine and kissed me gently. It was hellishly romantic even though he was taking my last bit of oxygen.

I pulled away to breathe.

'That was so good, Nik,' I panted, 'so good. But now, I need you inside me.' I moved to get back to the valuable work I was doing early but he stopped me.

'Let me do it this way,' he said, and gently turned me onto my stomach. He knelt behind me and pulled my hips up so I was kneeling. He reached for his jeans, grabbed a condom from the pocket and I heard the tear as he opened it and pulled it on.

'Okay?' he asked.

'Sure,' I assured him, but I didn't understand why he wanted to come this way when he couldn't see my face and I couldn't see his, especially for our first time. Was it a control thing? I didn't have a chance to think anymore, as he slowly moved into me. Holy crap, the pain.

'Slower Nik,' I cried and he immediately stopped. Keeping my balance, I grabbed his arm with my free hand and gripped tightly.

'Slower, sorry, slower,' Nik said, and eased off. His hands moved back to my hips and each movement so precise and deliberate. I arched, enjoying feeling him.

He groaned my name. 'Sah-sha, so good.'

I laughed because he summed it up so perfectly and then he wiped the smile from my face as he took me with several hard, fast moves. Groaning, aching, his wanting of me was so satisfying. I felt his whole body tense, and explode and he made a guttural sound like an animal sated. That was sexy too. He moved his hand up the outside of my body, wrapped me against him and with the other well-toned arm, lowered us onto the bed. I lay spooned into him; perfect.

'So good,' he said.

'So good,' I agreed, and we lay getting our breath. 'I'm so glad you persisted with us,' I said.

'I knew we'd be a perfect fit,' he said.

After some time, he reached for a tissue from the bed stand and pulled away to put the condom in it. He returned to hold me and we lay in silence. Eventually he spoke.

'I saw your ink but I didn't want to stop to ask... what does it mean,' he said. He ran his fingers over my chest and heart where the words lay, each move tingling my skin. I had the words 'Festina lente' tattooed over my heart.

'It's Latin, it means 'make haste slowly' – it is a reminder to fall in love slowly,' I said. 'My mother always uses that phrase and I'm a bit impulsive so I'm taking it on board.'

'Make haste slowly,' he repeated the words. 'Is it such a bad thing? Besides, can a leopard change his spots?'

I shrugged. 'Maybe not, but it's there to remind me.' I wanted to ask him something, but wasn't sure if I should yet. Then I remembered all the cloak and dagger shit I had gone through with Adam and I decided if we couldn't be upfront then we were screwed from the start. But before I could ask, he pulled me around and began to slowly kiss me again – God I loved how he did that, it was so sensual. I could have stayed that way all night except I could hear his stomach rumbling.

'You're hungry?' I asked.

'Starving,' Nik said.

'Didn't you eat after the game?' I frowned and turned to look at him.

'No, we showered and had a few drinks.'

'Nik!' I rolled my eyes, sitting up. 'You have to eat after a game. You can't run around for a couple of hours and not recharge. You are supposed to restore your body back to pre-game levels in the shortest possible time.'

Nik grinned at me. 'Is that so, coach?' he asked, reaching again down my body and I stopped him with an excellent tactical move.

I tried not to smile but failed. 'Yes,' I said, trying to stay serious with him. 'Doc told me. You need carbohydrates and fast. I can't believe the trainers let you guys leave without eating.'

'They had some pizza there and stuff, but I didn't need it then, I don't like to eat straight after a game – I had a sports drink.' He wised up. 'But yeah, you are right. I need to eat now. Plus you just took all my final energy supplies, I need resuscitation,' he said and dramatically fell back onto his back. I fell onto him.

'Right then. I'll give you the kiss of life and we'll go eat,' I said.

'Can we walk somewhere? I'm getting stiff,' he asked.

I gave him a raised eyebrow.

'In other areas,' he qualified his statement with a smile.

'There's a great steakhouse in walking distance.' I kissed him and jumped up before he could pull me back down. I raced naked down the stairs, and he grabbed his gear and followed.

I disappeared into the bathroom and he stopped at the doorway.

'You can come in,' I said, leaning into the shower to turn on the taps.

Nik walked in, laughed and stood with his hands on his hips looking around. He was so sexy and fully on display in my bathroom. I had designed it to be my dream bathroom – I liked smoked glass and mirrors and no obstructions and it was like a peek-a-boo room. You could see the silhouette of the person showering and there was a sizeable spa bath. It was definitely an apartment designed for a couple.

'This is very cool,' Nik said, and walked into the shower next to me. No door, just a smoky glass panel to step around and straight under a huge ten-inch square rain shower head that really wet you. Nik reached for me and I threatened him with the soap.

'No, you have to eat, we have to go. If you get faint or a bloody nose again, Doc will ban us from seeing each other,' I said, and passed him the soap. I slipped out of the shower, grabbed a towel to dry and left one out for Nik. I headed upstairs to change. Besides, if I stayed I would have to wash him down and explore those scars he didn't want to talk about and a few other areas. I soon realized that he took me from behind so I wouldn't ask him about them; it wasn't lost on me. But I wouldn't forget and next time we were intimate, I was going to see his face.

Chapter 14

'Don't move, Saffy,' I ordered my twin sister for the hundredth time. 'I swear, you'll end up with a lopsided wedding dress, it will look crap and you'll ruin my reputation before I get one,' I shook my head even though I couldn't really be cranky at her. The dress was looking fine and the cut was really perfect for Saffron. They had compromised – Saffy and Daniel – delaying the wedding for one year and traveling during that time. They had both given notice at work and would take off to Europe in a matter of weeks. I didn't want to think about how much I would miss her. Before then though, Saffron wanted the dress at a stage where she just needed a final fitting on her return.

'Saffy, please stand still or I'm going to have to tie you up,' I threatened her.

Saffron giggled. 'Sorry Sassy,' she said, but she couldn't stand still. I had pinned the dress together, it was heavy and she kept jabbing herself moving around with excitement – it was so good to see her happy. Saffy's fiancé wasn't allowed to be here but he would drop in later. On hand and not helping at all was our brother Ethan, along with Max and Saffy's best friend and the second bridesmaid Lilly. Lilly was more like Saffron than I was – they were both small brunettes and both a bit flaky. They believed in real love, poetry and pigs flying. Lilly was studying English literature; Lord knows what she was going to do with that.

I had left work right on five to get home to meet Saffy and co., so I didn't get to see Nik arrive for training and ogle him from the office window – I hated a missed opportunity. I would message him later and catch up. But now, I seriously had to focus on Saffron's dress and her wriggling wasn't helped by all the distractions – Max kept filling everyone's glasses with champagne, Lilly was creating home-made pizzas in the kitchen and Ethan played DJ – he had on some great jazz music. I had a mouthful of pins as I paced around Saffy on the bridal stage. Prada was giving me a sympathetic look from his perch above us, I was tempted to join him and refuse to come down. Add to this, all I could think about was one tall, gorgeous German – I couldn't sleep for thinking about him, damn him.

I didn't hear Lilly approach until she squealed and I jumped a mile high.

'You look so beautiful Saffy,' she gushed to my twin, 'even unfinished, it's beautiful.' She turned to me. 'You have such talent Sassy,' she said. 'Will you make my wedding dress one day too?' She glanced at Ethan as she said it. She didn't have a hope – Lilly was sweet but Ethan would need a much more challenging woman to keep him on his toes.

'I'd be honored, Lilly, especially if you chose one of my

designs and not a pattern,' I said with a sly glance to Saffron who rolled her eyes

'I've always wanted this style,' Saffron moaned.

'I know, I know,' I shushed her.

Lilly continued her focus on Ethan; worth a shot I guess.

'Ethan, has anyone ever told you that you look like Ryan Gosling, you know the actor?' she asked, batting her eyelids.

'No, no-one ever,' Ethan said, and I laughed. I tried not to, but he was so deadpan.

'Oh please Lilly, his head is big enough without telling him that,' I said, and he shot me a look that warned trouble. To add to the mayhem, there was a knock at the door. I looked at Ethan but he didn't turn the music down, it wasn't really that loud, so surely one of the neighbors wasn't freaking out.

'I'll get it,' Max said, making himself useful for the first time tonight. He opened the door and I heard him gasp a little. I was kneeling on the floor adjusting the hem of Saffy's dress and looked towards the door. There was a gorgeous athlete could-be model standing there – Nik. I grabbed the pins from my mouth and gave him a smile that said take me away from all this, or come in, one or the other.

He looked at me and his eyes lit up – we were alone in that space for a moment – and then it was like we both remembered there were other people in the room, and the room around us got suddenly noisier as everyone fussed over Nik. Max shook his hand, ushered him in and started introducing him to everyone, while I pushed up off my knees.

'Ah you are the best friend,' Nik said, shaking hands with Max. He turned to Ethan. 'And I thought you were Sah-sha's boyfriend, you had me worried,' he said, on being introduced to my brother.

Ethan grinned. 'God no, she's all yours, and good luck.'

I gave Ethan a smirk – I guess we were even now for my earlier Ryan Gosling comment. Lilly was looking at Nik like Adonis had just stepped into the room, she was so fickle – one minute fascinated by Ethan, the next absorbing the vision of Nik. She shook his hand and gazed at him in wonder, as if she wanted to paint him – she was always a bit ethereal our Lilly. I wanted to paint him in chocolate and lick it off, fuck there's an idea, keep that for later. Then my sister got her hooks into him. Poor Nik, but he did volunteer to come in.

'Ah, so you're Nik.' She smiled and shook his hand. 'You're quite beautiful, aren't you? Wow.'

I didn't think Nik – who spent a lot of time in the limelight – was capable of being really embarrassed but he went three shades of red and looked to me for rescue.

I grinned at him. 'He is beautiful,' I agreed, and he came over to me. He didn't seem to care that everyone else was there; he wrapped his arms around me, leaned down and kissed me. Again, the weirdest thing – as though it was just the two of us in the room and when we pulled apart, I realized for the first time tonight the room was quiet, everyone was watching us.

Nik looked around. 'Um, did I crash a party?' he asked.

'Hell no, you're very welcome,' Ethan said.

'Champagne?' Max asked.

'We've got beer,' Ethan said holding up his bottle.

'Yeah, a beer would be good, thank you,' Nik said. 'Sorry I came empty-handed.'

'Oh I doubt it,' I teased him, then I remembered we weren't alone and reddened. No need to give the family and friends fuel for gossip. I pulled out of his arms. 'I just need to help Saffy get out of this dress, so make yourself at home. You know your way around,' I said, trying to look more chilled and failing miserably.

'I'll message Daniel and tell him it is safe to come around now,' Saffron said, sending a message to her fiancé.

'I'll look after Nik,' Lilly said, brightly, and I knew she would. Not with the intention of stealing him, as Lilly was so sweet and lovely, she would just look after him – stare at him, size him up, try and work out how he ticked. A bell buzzed on the oven. 'Oh, the oven is ready, okay everyone I'm putting the pizzas in, you've got fifteen minutes,' she announced.

'I should go, so you can eat and see your friends,' Nik said.

'Don't be silly, I love you being here.' I grabbed his arm. 'I would have asked you but I didn't know if you'd cope with this lot or run screaming from me.'

Ethan laughed. 'Well that's nice isn't it?'

'Yeah don't be silly, we see each other all the time, the more the merrier,' Max said, handing Nik a beer. 'Besides, it's nice to see Sassy happy.'

I gave him a pained look. It was bad enough I felt as

though everyone was watching the two of us without Max letting on I'd been on another planet, planet joy. Nik's phone rang and he glanced at the screen.

'Ha, it's my best friend, he's here for a few weeks on business,' he said, 'you'll have to excuse me.'

'Here as in in-town? Ask him around if he's brave,' I said.

Nik smiled and took the call. He spoke in rapid German, so sexy to hear and watch. I'd have to get him to speak German to me in bed, don't care what he says, just say something. Saffron tugged my arm and I came back to reality and followed her into the guest room to help her out of the wedding dress.

'He's gorgeous,' Saffron whispered to me. I nodded, that I knew. 'This is just what you need Sassy, be open to it.'

I nodded again – she must have been talking with Ethan to say that. Saffron took my hand.

'Sassy, I love you and you're very lovable. I want to see you happy.'

I looked her in the eyes, my eyes – we weren't the kind of twins that felt each other's pain or knew when one of us was in trouble, but we had a deep connection and I would kill to protect her. 'I love you too,' I told her, 'but I'm just taking small steps here.'

'Of course,' she said. 'But everyone's vulnerable when they go into a relationship Sassy, everyone. Don't miss out because you're scared, it could be the best thing ever.'

'And if it is not?' I asked.

Saffron shrugged. 'Then you'll never die wondering.'

Brave words for someone who has had one major love

affair and is now marrying him – been there, done that, got the scars. I unpinned the back of her gown and she stepped out of the dress just wearing her underwear. I laid it carefully on the sofa while Saffron got dressed. When we came back out, Lilly had Ethan and Nik putting out plates and napkins for the pizza while Max was doing water glasses for everyone.

'Good job, Lilly,' I teased her, 'nice to see the boys doing something for a change.'

I ducked as they shot back barbs at me. Nik laughed, he looked so relaxed as though he belonged and he flicked me a glance which said he was happy to be there. I loved having the chance to watch him with my family and friends.

'Is your best friend coming?' I asked him.

'Yes, thanks. He's here for a week on business.'

'From Germany?' I asked, surprised Nik would be here and not with him if that was the case.

'No,' Nik assured me, 'He's been working in New York for six months, but he's on this side of the country just for a week.'

'I'll slow the pizzas down,' Lilly said, turning down the heat. 'This is turning into a party,' she said, excited. God bless Lilly, she had an endless supply of excitement. I might have to wear earplugs on Saffron's wedding day.

I suggested we put in an order for some Thai noodles from my local takeaway as well to feed the increasing population in my apartment. Max got on the job.

Fifteen minutes later Daniel, Saffron's fiancé, burst in.

'Safe?' he asked.

'All safe,' I agreed giving him a kiss on the cheek. 'Just don't go into the guest room, I've got the dress on the chair.'

'Wouldn't dream of it,' he said, greeting everyone, and kissing his fiancée. I was glad the love focus was a little off Nik and me, even though we were the novelty. Daniel seemed very impressed to meet Nik and congratulated him on his weekend game. They began to talk sport – sigh, men!

Ten minutes later there was another rap at the door and Nik excused himself to answer it; he back-slapped the man on the other side of the door and moved aside to let him in, closing it behind him.

'Ah, everyone, this is Anton,' Nik said.

Anton came bearing wine and beer and offered it up.

'Well, you can stay,' Ethan said, taking the drinks from him.

Nik then introduced Anton to each person and finished with me. Anton was tall too, but nothing on Nik's tall and gorgeous stature. Where was I? Oh yeah, Anton. He was probably just six foot or shy of it, light brown hair styled in a very corporate fashion and blue eyes, not as crystal blue as Nik's eyes. He wore silver-framed glasses and had the look of a banker – turns out he was a financier.

'So hello Sah-sha, you're the beauty who has captured Nik's heart,' he said with his lovely German accent. He shook my hand and Nik rolled his eyes, embarrassed. I grinned happily – it was Nik's turn for the big reveal, oh yeah, Anton coming around was a great idea. I realized that Lilly was staring at Anton now – so much male in one room.

Anton looked from Saffron to me. 'Wow, nothing alike

for twins. I would have thought you two were the twins,' he said looking from Lilly to Saffron.

'We get that all the time,' Saffron said.

'Sasha and Ethan look more alike,' Max added.

'Yes, we're the good-looking ones, we got the best genes but we don't like to rub it in,' Ethan teased and Saffron hit his arm. He handed Anton the same brand beer that he and Nik were drinking and the men sat on the sofa while the women fussed around... somehow we had taken on traditional domestic roles – that sucked.

'Ethan's one of three – triplets,' Saffy's fiancé Daniel told Anton, 'Ethan, Jason and Sam. You can just imagine what my first family meeting was like, each of them sizing me up and deciding if I was good enough to go out with Saffy or whether they'd kill me.'

I laughed. 'It wasn't that bad, Daniel.'

'It was. Your brother Jason asked did I have life insurance?' Daniel exclaimed and Saffron rubbed his arm.

'Well they all realized pretty quickly just how great you are,' she said.

'No we just realized that Daniel might be our only hope of getting rid of you while we can,' Ethan said, continuing the friendly banter.

'I'm not related to them,' Lilly said, for someone's benefit. Then the Thai takeaway arrived.

'Great, let's eat,' Lilly exclaimed.

I wanted to keep the atmosphere super chilled out; the music was good, the food smelled great, Max was just being Max, Lilly looked as though she was in heaven and Ethan and Saffron were really working hard at making Nik feel welcome – bless my siblings, so desperate to get me back on the horse, a German horse in this case.

But there wasn't enough air in the room for me; I just wanted everyone to leave so I could be with Nik and the glances we kept stealing told me he felt the same. It was such an amazing feeling being surrounded by everyone and having this one person in the room who I felt all this heat radiating from. Being separated by friends only enhanced my need to touch him. Memories of my first orgasm with him and lying naked in bed together didn't help me keep it together. I wanted more and I needed it, right now.

'He hasn't taken his eyes off you,' Saffron whispered in my ear.

I think it might have been mutual. I was trying not to look at him because I'd just be too horny and I might not be able to look away.

Lilly and Max put the pizzas and Thai on the center table and we perched around the room, on the rugs, on the sofas and the floor, helping ourselves. Nik moved beside me and our elbows touched as I served him. I swear he gave me an electric shock again.

He shrugged. 'Chemistry,' he explained it.

'So Anton,' my bestie, Max, began and I knew this would be trouble, 'now that you're here we can find out more about Nik and we can give you some inside information on Sasha.' He grinned at me. Right, note to self, Max was to be removed from the job of bestie. I saw Nik grimace too.

'How did you and Nik meet?' Max started his interrogation.

Anton finished a bite of his pizza. 'We went to school together, elementary and high school. I did Nik's math homework and he picked me every time we had to choose sides for sport,' he said, with a hint of amusement in his glance to Nik.

'Ah that's not quite true,' Nik said, abruptly interrupting the story. 'The part about the sport is true – Anton has no hand and eye coordination at all.' We all laughed and Anton gave him an unimpressed look. Nik continued, 'So it was a package deal. If I got picked for a team then they had to take Anton.'

'Like a two-for-one deal,' I suggested, 'you get an extra steak knife with the purchase.'

'Yeah, a blunt one in this case,' Nik teased his best friend. He gave as good as he got. 'As for you doing my math homework,' he said with a glance to Anton, 'I'm an accountant, how would that work?'

Anton laughed. 'Maybe it was English.'

'Oh his English is very good,' I said, 'his tongue has great command of – ' Before I could finish the sentence everyone burst out laughing.

'What?' I asked, and looked to Nik who smiled and shook his head at me.

'Of the language, his tongue has... oh never mind,' I said, trying not to smile.

Anton continued. 'Nik was also the only guy in senior year to take a supermodel to the formal – Lena Kruger, she was something.'

Ethan looked at Nik with new admiration. 'That's every

teenage boy's fantasy. I had to beg one of the twins' friends to come with me. I wasn't as handsome then.' He referred to Saffy and me like Mom and Dad do – the twins for the girls, the triplets for the boys. I grinned at the memory. Ethan had definitely grown into his face and body. At school, he was all angles.

Nik shrugged. 'She asked me, it was not a big deal.'

'He was a sports star then already,' Anton said.

Nik shook his head embarrassed and tried to change the subject but Anton held up his hand to him and kept going. 'Nik was playing in the top league at seventeen, and she was after a bit of extra publicity. I don't think she really had feelings for Nik,' Anton continued.

Nik frowned at him. 'Haven't you got to get back to the hotel or something? Early meeting tomorrow? Some phone calls to make?'

'No.' Anton shook his head, and got a round of laughs.

I studied Nik. He was hard to read, but at a guess, whenever Anton starting talking, Nik had a look of... fear in his eyes. What was he worried Anton was going to reveal? Prada strode past us and did a loop around Nik, settled beside him and lay down. Nik stroked him.

'That's impressive,' Saffron said. 'Prada doesn't like people, except Sassy.'

'I've always been good with pussies,' Nik said with a straight face and we all groaned.

Anton continued. 'So now, tell me about you Sah-sha, what has Nik gotten himself into? Obviously you have questionable taste in men,' Anton said, with a grin to Nik.

'Lucky I can't reach you,' Nik said, 'but I have a long memory.'

'Sasha's a fashion designer and a journalist and she works at the Saints with Nik,' Lilly piped up, stating the obvious. 'Although Nik is the first player she's ever dated, isn't that right, Sassy?'

'It's the first one she's got right for a long time,' Max added, sweetly.

I rolled my eyes; friends, who needs them?

'We're very happy to meet you Nik, because seriously Sassy was just working herself into old age. So boring, no life...' Saffron was saying.

'Hold up, I'm here!' I reminded them. I turned to Nik. 'Haven't we got somewhere we've got to be?' I asked him.

He glanced upstairs to my bedroom. 'Yes, and look at the time.'

'Nice try, but tomorrow is a school day so no late night for you two,' Ethan said. 'Besides Nik has to drop Anton home to the hotel, can't have a guest taking a taxi.'

I looked at my sensible brother who just prevented me having great sex. He'd pay for that.

*****

Ethan was the last to leave and he hovered to give me a hand cleaning up. I suspected he wanted to tell me something.

'I like him, Sassy, he's a good guy and he's clearly mad about you, he kept sneaking glances at you all night,' he said. Music to my ears.

'The marks, you saw them?' I asked.

Ethan nodded. He folded his arms and leaned back on the kitchen island as I wiped the last of the plates.

'I'm not one hundred percent sure, but I'm about ninety percent – I've seen that before on some of my patients, they're cigarette burn scars,' Ethan said, in a quiet voice.

I wheeled around to look at him. 'Wait, you're telling me that the scars Nik has on his chest and back are from someone putting out a cigarette on him?' Tears raced to my eyes and I felt physically sick. I knew this sort of thing happened but to see it on someone you... well like-love, I couldn't get my head around it.

Ethan pulled me in for a hug. I let him, before pulling away.

'I'm okay, really,' I said, 'just a bit blown away. How old are they?'

Ethan shrugged. 'I don't know, but given the size of Nik now, I doubt anyone could do that to him and live to tell. You said he was an orphan?'

I nodded.

'Then I suspect he didn't have a happy childhood, Sassy. Did he have a foster family or did he grow up in an institution?' Ethan asked.

'I don't know,' I said, honestly. 'I didn't ask more questions because he shut down. I've only seen the marks up close once,' I said, knowing Ethan would get my meaning. 'Nik grabbed my hand when I went to touch one of the scars and then he shut down. He wouldn't let me see and he diverted the topic every time.'

Ethan nodded.

'What should I do?' I asked.

'Nothing, especially nothing,' Ethan said.

I frowned. 'I don't want to spend my life doing it doggy style or having him wear a shirt.'

Ethan grimaced. 'Yeah thanks, more information than I really needed. It's his call when he tells you, if he tells you.'

'Fair enough,' I said, knowing I wouldn't like Nik asking me about Adam if I wasn't ready to talk.

Ethan pulled on his chin as he thought. 'Um, I don't think it was any coincidence either that Nik's friend showed up just as you two are hotting up. He's working in New York City and now he suddenly had business here on the other side of the country?'

'You think he's checking me out?' I asked, astounded. 'It's a long way to come to check me out.'

Ethan shook his head. 'Not that far to come compared to Germany and he was in the country. So, yeah, I do think that's why he's here. I'm guessing Nik has no-one in the world but a few close friends?'

'I guess so. His next of kin is Anton,' I said.

'How do you know about his next of kin?' Ethan asked.

'Insider information,' I told him, touching my nose.

'Hmm. You know how close our family is and how loyal you and Max are to each other. Imagine if Max was an orphan and you were his closest friend, his family more or less and had been since school...'

'I'd be screening any one who came into his life to make sure they treated him right,' I said.

'Exactly,' Ethan said. 'Especially if you knew he had been

mistreated. These guys have known each other for years and sounds like they've had each other's back even at school. I think Anton's looking after his 'brother' in the true sense of the word.'

I nodded, thinking.

'So I shouldn't raise the subject? I should just ignore the scars?' I asked.

'That's just my opinion from the experience I've had – you need to let him tell you when he is ready to trust you. He may never tell you. He might want to bury that part of his life. But don't force it Sassy, you'll push him away.'

'How could anyone do that to a kid?' I asked.

'Beats me, but they do and worse.'

This time, I reached out and squeezed my brother's arm. 'I forgot how much you see, I'm sorry.'

'I signed up for it,' he reminded me. He glanced at his watch. 'Got to go, thanks for tonight.'

'You know Lilly is still in love with you?' I teased him.

'Sweet Lilly, I'd eat her for breakfast.' Ethan sighed. I saw him out and returned to the kitchen to make a tea. I took it to the sofa, sat and thought about the evening. Prada joined me and I stroked his sleek, black coat.

I exhaled. Wow, what had I got here? This connection that Nik felt, that he felt right from the start, it was a little more intense than I thought and carried a lot more responsibility. I had the sudden urge to want to make the rest of his life so happy, so secure and full of love. Surround him with kids and family and all the things he didn't have.

I sighed. Boy did Nik have the wrong girl.

Chapter 15

What the fuck was going on in the universe? Good grief – my ex-husband Adam, in between flirting with models at the bridal expo, was still messaging me and clearly finding me much more attractive now that we're divorced, what was that about? Now, Dan whom I have known for a hundred and five years – okay five years at least – has suddenly decided it's time to ask me out. If Nik found out his jaw would be locked for a week and I'd never get any decent kissing action. Crap!

I just got to work on Tuesday morning after a great impromptu gathering last night with Nik and our friends when at ten o'clock, a bunch of flowers arrived. Actually they weren't flowers, technically it was a chocolate posy – a flower bouquet made of chocolates.

Alice's face dropped with disappointment as Suzie our receptionist brought them in and put them in front of me – Tomás had never sent flowers to Alice, he was more of an in-person guy – and Kay had long given up on getting flowers unless it was her anniversary.

'Lucky you,' Alice sighed admiring the arrangement until she realized they were chocolates.

'O.M.G., it's chocolate, I think we should test them now, make sure they're okay' she teased.

I grinned like the Cheshire cat thinking they were from Nik until I read the card. My face dropped. Damn I'd be no good at poker, I should have faked it but I didn't get my reactions in order in time. The card read: *We should catch up, Dan.*

'What's wrong?' Alice said.

'They're from Dan… a journo I saw on Sunday. I've known him for years and now he wants to catch up. I don't get it,' I said, still looking at the card as if the words might dissolve and Nik's message would appear. From Dan. Yep, that Dan – Dan who has known me since university and never looked twice at me. Did I wave hello in a more fascinating way than usual on the weekend at the game? Did sitting next to him in the media box take on a whole new significance this weekend and I missed it? I've said it before and I'll say it again, what the fuck? It seems Dan dropped the posy bouquet in but I was on the phone so he headed off. I bet it was re-gifted… I know Dan, he doesn't spend a dollar without knowing there's a possible return.

'I bet there's a chocolate posy promotion at K-Talk, and these are leftovers,' I said, offering them to Kay and Alice.

'That's terrible, Sasha.' Kay shook her head and scolded me, but happily took two. 'I'm sure he's a lovely young man who has just come to appreciate your charms.'

I snorted. 'Yes, well can't blame him,' I teased her. Alice

took a couple and hoarded one for later – I've noticed she was a bit of a food hoarder… no wonder the office had mice.

Why is it that women rarely get flowers from the one they want to get them from? Wow, how ungrateful did I sound, but it's a truth universally acknowledged, with apologies to Jane Austen. If you took a poll of every girl on the planet, I bet they'd say they've had flowers from the wrong guy. I'm raving again, great.

'Maybe he's just broken up with someone, Sash,' Kay said.

I clicked my fingers at her. 'I bet you are right, Kay, and now he's looking at what's in his playing field.'

'Well you're not available,' Alice reminded me.

'I know.' I grinned, then sobered up quickly. 'If Nik comes in, these are not mine,' I said.

'Well they're not mine,' Alice added.

We both looked at Kay and she smiled. Bless her.

'Where's the coffee van?' Jim bellowed from the other side of the wall. I rolled my eyes as Alice giggled. We all knew the feeling. I was in a total relaxed state – we had a bye this weekend which meant less pressure on me, no weekend work… not that we minded because game day was so exciting and I got longer with Nik. I mused… that might be why Anton arrived, because it was a weekend without a game. Perhaps Ethan was wrong about him checking up on me and he was just taking the opportunity to catch up with Nik – either way, I was taking Nik shopping this weekend, hell yeah!

The Russian came out of his office and went past us; we all looked up to watch the moving scenery. Not until he got well past us and to the door did he say, 'coffee van's here ladies.' Did I mention The Russian sucks? Alice and I rose to get the morning run for the marketing team. If Jim didn't get his soon he was going to start glue sniffing. This time, I had my purse ready… the others could fix me up later. I jumped in queue while Alice confirmed orders in the office and I was right behind The Russian and before Shayne. Yep, I'm slick and getting slicker.

I narrowed my eyes at The Russian. 'So big guy, how did you know the van was coming?'

He smiled at me, his dark eyes narrowing. 'I have my sources.'

'Bullshit, that's my line,' I told him. 'You've bribed our coffee lady to message you, haven't you?'

Shayne was grinning as he watched the two of us sparring.

'You won't win, Sasha,' Shayne said, 'wall by build, wall by nature.' He took in The Russian.

'Hmph,' I said, or something similar. Alice arrived beside me and Shayne arced up.

'Are you jumping queue Alice?' he said.

'Hell no, Shayne. Me? Never. I'm just bringing the cash to Sash,' she said, handing over Kay and Jim's coffee order.

'You're all too good at this for me.' Shayne shook his head. 'I'm going to need a system. Russian, will you get my coffee so I can get back to work and making our team great?'

The Russian grinned while Alice and I groaned.

'That's pathetic, Shayne,' I said.

'Yeah,' he agreed and gave The Russian his money for a latte.

'Pathetic!' I called after him and he gave me a wave as he left to return to the office.

I turned back and The Russian was looking at me. 'Who are the flowers from Sash?'

'Dan, the journo,' Alice piped up then covered her mouth. My eyes went huge.

The Russian laughed. 'You'd make a great spy Alice. Better hope Tomás has no secrets.'

I groaned and Alice gave me a sympathetic look. 'Sorry Sash,' she said, grimacing.

The Russian shook his head. 'That'll get back.'

'They're not flowers, they're chocolates, re-gifted chocolates I suspect, and it can't get back, Russian,' I said to him. 'You know Dan, so do I, he's been around forever and I'm so not interested. He's just trying his luck... probably newly single.'

The Russian nodded. 'Yeah wouldn't want to see the Kaiser angry, never seen that actually,' he said with renewed interest.

'Let's not see it,' I suggested. Damn my ex, Adam; damn Dan – although it was a lovely thought; but in general sometimes men just sucked and not in the best way.

*****

When I took a break for lunch, I looked over my shoulder, checked there was no one around, and did a quick online search on Nik. There were heaps of press clippings, great photos, awards, wonder boy stories and pics of him with beautiful women in Berlin – so glad I saw those. I could only read the articles that were in English but there was no mention of his family. I found a long interview he did just before he came to the States where he talked about his first coach being his inspiration. I read through it; at thirteen he had moved in with the coach and his wife when signed in the junior league and they managed his early career. Interesting. Not one mention of his family in that article either or where he had grown up. There were a couple of social shots with Anton in them along with a handful with women. Hmm.

What's your story Nik? I want to be very careful not to accidentally break you.

Chapter 16

I needn't have worried about being the one to break Nik because it appears it was The Russian's turn this time, the universe had let me off the hook. I only heard about it second-hand but Alice came rushing in after lunch and dragged me to the office window overlooking our playing grounds. Up near the training rooms was an ambulance, and all the players along with Doc and coach Johan were milling around.

'What the hell is going on?' I asked.

Alice explained: 'I just pulled into the parking lot and Tomás saw me and came over because I was worried. Johan was holding a game review meeting just before lunch...'

'I know, Nik said it would go for about two hours and then they had a compulsory lunch for team bonding as he called it.'

Alice nodded and we watched as the ambulance drove out of the grounds. The players started heading to their cars except for The Russian and Buzz who went back into the building with Shayne and Johan. Alice turned to me.

'Well Russian and Buzz got into a fight. I don't know what it was about but they went at each other,' Alice said.

'Wow, must have been major because it takes a lot to rile Russian, he doesn't get worked up about anything,' I said. I shook my head.

Alice agreed. 'Buzz is nuts to annoy The Russian, you don't want to stir a sleeping giant. Anyway, they went at it. Unfortunately Harry and Nik entered as The Russian and Buzz slammed each other against the wall. You know Harry kind of hero worships Nik a bit and Lucas too. I think they're both very supportive of him, helping him along,' Alice said getting off subject.

'Are Nik and Harry okay?' I pushed her.

'Sort of. Nik was rammed into the wall and got a mild concussion. Tomás said something about low blood pressure too, but he was out cold for a few minutes and Harry might have a broken arm,' she finished.

I gasped. 'That was Nik and Harry going off in the ambulance?'

She nodded. 'Nik's okay though, he's woken up; they're just going to run some checks on him.'

I shook my head. 'That's crazy and what if Harry's season is over because of in-club fighting? Wait until I see The Russian.' I looked to the oval and saw him, with his business partner, Ed, and Shayne walking back towards our office admin area. Several of the club physical therapists followed them. What was it with The Russian and Buzz?

Alice continued like a good gossiper. 'Tomás said Russian

feels really bad about it, but Buzz is totally flippant,' Alice added.

'Hmm, this could be big trouble for Buzz,' I said, lowering my voice. 'Before you came to the club, he's had warnings for in-club fighting, missing training, drinking when he shouldn't.' I exhaled. 'Johan will be beside himself.'

We heard The Russian coming and he must have heard my last comment.

'Johan is fucking furious,' The Russian growled, 'and so am I. Bad enough we get injuries on the field but from each other, it's not on.'

'Lot of money in this game, careers at stake, and we can't afford to have players out,' Ed, his business partner said, coming up behind him and moving past to return to their Saints' Security office.

The Russian breathed out. 'I'm sorry Sash about your man, it was never about him, just bad timing. Buzz is a dickhead.'

I nodded. 'Where have they taken Nik and Harry?'

'St. Andrews hospital, I'm going up now. Want a lift?' he asked.

'No, I'll go straight after work if you think he's okay?' I said, knowing they'd run tests on Nik for a while first and I might not get access to him immediately. I didn't even have Anton's number to let him know but I guess they would have contacted him or Nik's manager who might contact Anton.

'He'll be fine. We won't though,' The Russian glanced out to the oval. 'With the bye this weekend we had no training tomorrow, but Johan has just called a session. We're going to be whipped.' He sighed and walked to his office.

I looked at Alice. 'At least I didn't injure Nik this time,' I said.

'Yeah, but be careful at the hospital,' she said, in all seriousness. I gave her a special look.

*****

Just after five-thirty, I arrived at the hospital and found Nik asleep in pale blue hospital-issued pajamas in a private room – so cute. He was propped up, had a drip in his arm and his usually tanned faced looked a little whiter than usual. Anton was sitting reading the newspaper in the corner and grinned on seeing me. He rose. He was in a suit but his jacket hung over the back of the chair.

'Hello Sah-sha,' he whispered and kissed me on the cheek, his German accent as strong as Nik's inflections.

I took his hand, pleased to see him. 'Hi Anton, how is he?' I said in a quiet voice glancing at the patient.

'He'll be fine, so will Harry – not a break, just a sprain. Wrong place, wrong time,' Anton said.

'What a relief they are both okay – they don't call Russian the wall for nothing.' I sighed. 'It's good to see you again,' I smiled at him, releasing his hand. 'I didn't know how to reach you to let you know about Nik and I wasn't sure when you go back to New York.'

'Thanks, his manager called me. I leave tomorrow,' he said. He pulled the two visitors' chairs together near the

160

door, a little farther away from Nik so we wouldn't disturb him. We sat down and I gave him a surprised look.

'I thought you might be staying for his bye weekend to catch up.'

'Ah no, just for a few days. I believe he has plans for the weekend since he has it off … heading away for a few days,' Anton said, giving me a mysterious look like I should know that – maybe Nik was going away for the weekend and I just thought we'd spend it together shopping for him, eating out and dining on each other! I felt a wave of disappointment and anger at myself for expecting too much from men, I always do that. I should learn to expect nothing, then I'd never be disappointed. I made a note to talk with myself about that later.

I glanced over on hearing Nik stir but he didn't wake up. He looked so vulnerable lying in the bed and very kissable, I just wanted to lift up the sheet and get in beside him.

'He's a bit high, something in that drip is relaxing him,' Anton said, looking to Nik.

'Oh good, I might get some home truths.'

Anton studied me.

'Can we talk?' I asked, and he nodded. I leaned back in the chair. 'I'm guessing your trip here is to check up on me.'

Anton looked surprised and then he smiled. 'Nik said you were as direct as he was, a good thing I think.'

I nodded and smiled, but didn't speak waiting for his answer.

'I did have some business here, but yes, I guess I do take on the responsibility of looking after Nik. I am a few months older than him after all,' he said, with a small smile. 'I thought I could do the business and meet you at the same time.'

'Oh I think it goes deeper than that,' I teased him, but I really wanted the truth without being authoritative. Come on Anton, spill it. 'You grew up together?'

Anton nodded. 'Nik didn't have the happiest of childhoods and when he could, he spent a lot of time at my house when we were growing up. We were both skinny kids. Nik didn't shoot up until he was about fourteen and then he grew about a foot a week.'

I smiled at the thought.

'He could defend himself then, but before that well... anyway he had a real talent for soccer, it was noticed early and he was a school champion and district champion. He got signed up as a rookie for the major leagues – he was one of the youngest ever recruits.'

We glanced at Nik again as he groaned but didn't wake up.

Anton continued. 'The coach of the State squad and his wife billeted him, you know let him stay and he spent half his day at school and half at training. Sebastian and Britta – they were very good to him, treated him like a son, still do. He went on to college on a scholarship and earned more before he finished college than most of us will see in our working lives.'

I listened intently and finished for him. 'So when everyone wanted a piece of him, you were one of the few that wanted nothing more than friendship and he trusts you?'

'And I trust him,' he said. 'So when he says he's fallen in... has he said...?'

'No,' I nipped Anton's love comment in the bud.

'Well, I assure you, he's on the trip and when he told me that, I just wanted to check that you were sincere I guess.'

'Did I pass?' I asked Anton.

He grinned. 'You are lovely Sah-sha, direct, sincere, not after anything more than his returned affection from what I can tell. I couldn't ask for more for him.'

I smiled my thanks, not that I needed Anton's endorsement and I kind of resented being checked out just a bit, but I appreciated his concern for Nik.

Anton cleared his throat quietly. 'He's a bit insecure with you if you don't mind me saying. He said you are not sure of your feelings for him.'

I nodded. 'I'm recently divorced and I've learned a few lessons,' I explained. 'I know how I feel about Nik, I just wish that he wasn't a player and I wish I met him maybe in a year or two. I'm finding my feet again.'

'I understand,' Anton said. 'Odd though. Most women would love that he's a player.'

'I work there full time; I don't really want to date a player... makes it messy.' I frowned.

'He won't always be a player and you won't always work there,' Anton said. 'In a few years you could both be on very different journeys, together.'

'That's true.' I brightened at the thought.

'Plus, given you've been through a bit, maybe you both deserve a bit of happiness. But let me ask you, Sah-sha...

what do you know of Nik?' Anton said, with a quick glance to the bed.

I looked over at Nik and returned my gaze to Anton. 'I know what he has told me, I know he is very black and white. I wouldn't have put us together, but Nik has no doubts. And... I've seen the scars.'

Anton nodded.

'Is there anything I should know now or about his past?' I asked, my eyes narrowing on Anton as I tried to read him.

He shook his head. 'His past is... well his story to tell. But Sah-sha, you appear to be surrounded by love, grew up in a loving family. Nik has me, Sebastian and Britta. He is looking for that relationship that will fill him and I'm not sure if he knows how to trust or love; maybe he will rush in because he wants it so much... but you can work through that with him.' He inhaled and then tapped my knee with his webbed fingers. 'I guess if I could ask one thing of you?'

I nodded, inviting him to ask me.

'Be patient. What you take for granted could scare the hell out of him.'

'Don't worry,' I promised him with a smile, 'I think that is mutual.'

We heard Nik move and we turned to look at him. He lay watching us, his eyes open and focusing on me, his eyes lit up.

'Sah-sha, you're here,' he said in a groggy voice. Anton and I rose and went to his bedside. I reached for his hand.

'This time you can't blame me,' I teased him. 'Can't stay out of a fight huh?'

'I think the fight came to me,' he said. 'I was standing and then I wasn't. It was like Russian was a bowling ball hurtling towards me.'

'How are you feeling now, Nik?' Anton asked.

'Very relaxed. This is a good space to be in,' he said, glancing to the intravenous line in his arm. 'We should come here more, you should come here with me Sah-sha.'

Anton smiled. 'Well I'm going to go back to the hotel and shower. It's been a long day. I'll drop in and see you tomorrow morning Nik.'

'Okay Ant, thanks for being here.' He drifted off for a minute while Anton gathered his coat, and then he re-woke with a start, his gaze falling on Anton. 'Is it safe?' he asked.

Anton's eyes flicked to mine and back to Nik. 'It's safe here,' he said and patted Nik's arm.

'Good,' Nik said. He said something in German and Anton moved closer to the bed again. He tried to get Nik to look at him and focus. They were speaking in German and I stood back to give them some privacy even though I didn't understand them, then Nik drifted off again.

'I'm sorry about that Sah-sha,' Anton said, looking uncomfortable.

'Where do the scars come from, Anton?' I asked him directly.

'The scars...' Anton looked to Nik, debating whether to tell me.

'Ethan – you met my brother, is a counselor. He recognized them and Nik wouldn't let me see them when we were last together. He tried to hide them. Did his foster parents do that?' I asked.

Anton still wouldn't meet my eyes. He was watching Nik as though waiting for him to wake and answer the question. 'He was fostered for a number of years. When he was seven, eight maybe, well one of his foster fathers... they removed Nik once they realized.'

I swallowed and looked at Nik. I was angry and sad. 'What did he mean by safe?'

'He's just a bit confused about where he is, a flashback you might call it. He's okay, don't worry,' Anton assured me. 'I'll go now. It was good to meet you. I'm pleased Nik has you.'

I kissed him on the cheek and thanked him, watching him leave. I turned back to Nik and took his hand. Ten minutes later he opened his eyes again and looked at me with a surprised expression as though he had never seen me.

'You look very beautiful, Sah-sha. I love your hat,' he said, admiring my soft felt brimmed hat.

'I was worried,' I said, stroking his hand. 'I'm going to have to kill Russian.'

Nik smiled. 'It's not his fault, just bad timing. I'm really fine, just a concussion. Is Harry okay? Is Johan angry?' he asked after the coach, his words slow and slurred.

I nodded. 'Harry has a sprained arm, but at least it is not broken. As for Coach, he's pissed off and Doc is super angry, but neither of them with you.'

'Can we go now, back to your place?' he asked. 'I want to watch you shower behind the glass.'

I smiled and leaned in, placing my cheek next to his.

'Soon,' I agreed.

'I love you Sah-sha,' he said, and I froze. I looked up at him but his eyes were closed and his breathing steady, as he had drifted off again.

'I love you too, Nik,' I whispered. Wow, I was getting brave, even if I was the only one to hear me say that.

Chapter 17

It was awful to see and kind of hot too – The Russian was right, the coach was working their asses into the ground. Alice and I watched from the office window. Instead of enjoying the training break, the whole team was punished for Buzz and The Russian's in-house fighting – probably because it wasn't the first time and Johan was trying to establish it would be the last. I could see from afar that Doc and the PT guys were pulling Nik and Harry out of the mix a fair bit to allow for their recovery.

A few journos arrived and after getting the call from reception to announce them, I left Alice and escorted them to the grounds. Johan, Shayne and I agreed earlier on the official line – the in-house fighting was to be denied and we were going with the coach giving them one final workout before letting them have four days off for the bye. I escorted the journos to the field and they took some pics, had a chat with Johan and Shayne, who watered down the injuries as just the usual fallout from a game.

I tried not to look at Nik but it was impossible, what's a girl to do? He was there training lightly and looking gorgeous, a sweat sheen on his body, and standing out in the pack. Fuck he was hot, and now I was. He glanced up at me and gave me a sexy stare with just the hint of a smile. Best not to smile when training – the coach takes that as evidence that you're not working hard enough and will double your load.

Lucas was counting down the crunches. I could feel my body clenching in supportive agony... they would need the four days to recover. The Russian at least had the good grace to look humble, Buzz on the other hand just looked defiant – I doubted he would be re-signed at the end of the season on his behavior alone, unless he turned up such a brilliant few games that he made himself indispensable.

I gave Shayne a sign that I was returning to the office and leaving the journos in his care which was our normal procedure if the media wanted to stay on for training. I took another quick peek at Nik to get my fill of him and moved on.

*****

Wednesday night and we were out for dinner. I hadn't broached the subject of the weekend bye yet and if Nik was free to hang out, but I assumed he had already made plans from what Anton said. I was kind of leaving it open in case he hadn't. God I hated that I did that, but I couldn't help myself. I really was an all-in or all-out person when it came to relationships, just like I had been with Adam. You would think I would learn.

I took a sip of my green tea and looked at the gorgeous German man opposite me.

'Nik, I know this is only the second restaurant we've tried,' I said getting serious, 'but if we were to keep eating out like this, how long until you go broke and we have to go back to my grilled cheeses and cheap wine for dinner?'

It was my turn to choose a restaurant and I had selected Japanese tonight – we had established that we both loved our food and eating out. Trying some of the better places in town was just a bonus that I couldn't have afforded on my own – we shared fresh sushi for starters and were now onto teriyaki chicken and yakizakana or translation, grilled fish.

Nik – looking divine in black suit pants and a light gray knit pullover – did the calculation in his head. I just loved watching him, he was so beautiful. I could almost hear his accountant brain doing the math.

'Well, Sah-sha, If you exhaust me with your sexual demands so that I can only play out my two-year contract with the Saints; and we don't spend money on anything else but eating out, we'll be right for ninety-six years at this rate,' he said.

My eyes widened. 'Wow, so I can order a cola then?'

'That will make it ninety-five years, but if you want to be reckless…' he shrugged. 'We haven't added your potential designer income. You might end up supporting me if I retire injured.'

I gave him a shocked expression. 'No way am I doing that,' I said, and he laughed.

'I'll return all favors in kind,' he said.

'Okay, done,' I agreed.

'Wow, that was the easiest contract I've ever negotiated.' Nik looked surprised, using his chopsticks to devour a mouthful of steamed rice.

'Niklas, are you calling me easy?' I asked.

He reached for his green tea and swallowed a sip. 'I think you trapped me Sah-sha,' he said.

'I think I did,' I agreed. 'Are you staying the night with me?'

He smiled, my question taking him by surprise. 'I was hoping to, yes. Is that okay?'

I nodded. 'Of course.' I lowered my voice and leaned in close to him. 'I want to see your face when we make love tonight.'

He looked away from me, his gaze returning to his green tea. 'Sure, if you like,' he said, with an attempt to keep his voice nonchalant but I could see he was in panic mode, his Adam's apple bobbing as he swallowed down his fear.

'I won't ask about the scars, I promise,' I whispered.

He nodded but didn't look at me. And then I saw Tomás and Alice enter. I waved to Alice and they came over.

'Hey, didn't know you were going to be here?' Alice said.

'Alice, Tango,' Nik greeted them.

'Hey Kaiser, Sass…sha, it's not my first choice,' Tomás said, and he didn't look happy. 'I'll have to have a meal when I get home.' He rolled his eyes and Alice hit his arm. Nik laughed.

'Why don't guys like Japanese?' I asked.

'Because it's light, and fish and pickle stuff,' Tomás answered.

'I like it,' Nik said. 'So well prepared and fresh.'

I looked at him with appreciative eyes. He was a man of good taste.

'Want to join us?' Alice asked.

'No,' Nik said, flatly. 'But thanks.'

Alice looked put out, Tomás grinned at Nik's directness and I tried to smooth it over.

'He wants me to go under the table soon,' I shrugged to Alice, 'and you don't want to see that.'

Tomás laughed again. Bless him for having a sense of humor while Alice looked a mixture of mortified and disbelieving. Nik on the hand looked as though I had just had the best idea since the missionary position was deemed boring.

'See you around the club,' Tomás said, and grabbed Alice's hand, departing.

'Well...' Nik said.

'Well, have you tried this teriyaki chicken?' I asked putting a piece directly in line with his lips. He snapped it off my chopsticks.

'Mm,' he said, with appreciation. 'When are you doing it? Going under the table?' His eyes were wide and from the way he shuffled in his seat I'm guessing he was up for it.

'Nah, I just said that so we could sit by ourselves,' I teased him.

'No Sarsh, come on, I've just had a concussion. You need to check everything is in working order,' he moaned.

I shook my head at him. 'I have four words for you, Nik...'

His eyes lit up with anticipation. 'Okay?'

'Pass the steamed rice.'

He groaned and I laughed.

'I promise to take an inventory of your body and make sure everything is working as soon as we get to my bed,' I said. 'Okay?'

'If under the table is out of the question, I guess that will be fine,' he said. 'That is a beautiful dress, Sah-sha.' He ran his eye from my neck to the table line.

'Thanks, again.' He had told me that a few times. I designed it. It's one of my favorite designs – a black button down long sleeve dress with a white collar and white wrist sleeve cuffs. It went to below the knees and I wore black knee-length boots with it.

'What have you got on underneath?' he teased.

'Nothing,' I said, sipping my green tea. Considerate as I am, I had worn a dress that buttoned right down the front with nothing underneath but my knee-high boots. And I mean nothing.

Nik stopped and stared at me. 'But lingerie, what lingerie do you have underneath?'

I shook my head. 'None.'

'Fuck me,' he whispered. 'Finished?'

Men. I suggested we order dessert.

*****

My feet didn't touch the ground from the moment we came

through my front door and we arrived in my bedroom. Praise be the patron saint of fit men – Nik picked me up in the hallway, ran up the stairs to my loft bedroom with me in his arms and had me in the bedroom before I had time to truly appreciate his muscles involved in the exercise. Nik called out hello to Prada as we went up the stairs, bless him, he was earning serious brownie points. He put me down on the edge of the bed.

'Tonight Sah-sha is the night where we don't muck around, so don't move,' he ordered, not taking his eyes off me as I sat on the edge of the bed. I don't think he believed I was completely naked beneath my dress – I deliberately went commando, knowing I could slip the fact in somewhere during the night. He slipped off his knitted jumper, the white T-shirt under it, pushed off his shoes and socks, undid his belt and then looked at me. I could see the scars on his body and the tatts down his arm and side, across his ribs. I tried not to focus on the scars; I didn't need him freaking out, I just wanted us to have sex tonight.

'I want to unwrap you, like a present,' he said and strode over with his sexy tailored pants on and naked chest. He leaned down and unzipped my boots, taking off each one before standing again, and reaching for me.

'Pants first,' I said, unzipping him as they were right in my eye line. He grabbed a condom from the pocket, put it on the drawer beside the bed and stepped out of his black trousers. He threw them over a chair and turned back to find me studying his package, back to front.

He smiled. 'Okay?'

'Oh yes,' I nodded enthusiastically. Tonight he had on black boxer briefs with a white waistband – very nice. I wanted to rush in case we were interrupted by some sort of karma, like jilted sisters, concussion, bloody noses, low blood pressure or visiting friends!

He reached down and lifted me from under my elbows, raising me to standing height. He took a deep breath and undid the first button on my dress, working his way down. I heard the sharp intake of his breath as he undid the final button that revealed me as completely naked.

'Magnificent Sah-sha,' he said, with a slow smile. I swear the man was panting slightly. He pulled the dress back off my shoulders, threw it over his pants on the chair, and looked at me completely naked in front of him.

He reached for me, his fingers stroked over my hips, up through the hourglass of my waist, to my breasts before sending shivers racing through my nerve endings.

'I can't believe you were naked under that dress,' he said.

'I thought going out without underwear was normal,' I said as innocently as I could muster.

He smiled and then took complete control.

It was unbelievable, the sensations, his sensitivity, being controlled by Nik's large hands, not able to move an inch, my whole body was bucking. I came in rush of light and ecstasy, and I think I screamed Nik and God's name several times. I was panting, but he didn't give me time to come down, there was an urgency about tonight. He kept me lying on my stomach, I heard the condom tear and he was pushing against me to enter me from behind again.

Before I could stop him, he was sliding in and my body was welcoming him – pleasure and pain. I moaned, wanting more, loving the feeling of being one. As my body braced with total pleasure, he hissed my name through clenched teeth and came, his frame vibrating and his grip on me so tight I could barely breathe. We worked through it, letting it rise and flow and then I felt his weight on me as he slumped forward, holding his weight but pushing us both flat on the bed. I don't know how long we stayed there but I felt him pull out, dispose of the condom and return to hold me. When I eventually opened my eyes and turned to face him, his crystal blue eyes were watching me.

'I didn't think I was going to make it home after you told me you had nothing under that dress,' he said, softly.

'I admire your control,' I teased him. 'That Nik, was unbelievable.' I smiled.

'What a great end to a great night.' He sighed.

It hadn't been lost on me that yet again, Nik didn't want me to see his scars.

I jostled and pushed him on his back. I knew he wasn't comfortable being exposed completely naked front on but it was time to tackle this. I saw his eyes flick to where his T-shirt lay over a chair but that was not going to happen. I leaned up on one elbow and began to trail my fingers over his tanned chest.

I looked at his largest tattoo: a detailed Celtic design sun with the German words '*Untergegangen um wieder zu steigen*' inked below it.

'What does that mean?' I asked pronouncing it awkwardly.

Nik laughed at my pronunciation and said it quickly and fluidly. 'It means 'set to rise again', he translated it for me. I noticed Nik's breathing was jagged as he waited for my questions.

'That's beautiful, but you use a lot of words for a short sentence,' I said.

Nik grinned. 'We Germans like our words long.'

'Yes, long is good,' I agreed, teasing him. 'Why the sun?'

'The sun gives light to guide through dark times... the tatt is about survival,' he said, and I nodded, not pushing it.

He took my hand and stopped my journey across his chest.

'We both don't have to work this weekend,' he said, referring to his playing and my Saints' media work.

Ah here it comes, at least he brought it up.

'We are free spirits,' I agreed.

'Have you planned anything?' he asked.

'Not yet, I haven't given it much thought,' I said, as casually as I could muster.

'I meant to ask you earlier, but I forgot with Russian knocking me out... I booked a weekend away for us if that's okay? I can cancel it if you don't want to go, but do you think you could take Friday off if Jim will let you?'

'Really? A weekend away!' I almost squealed, so unlike me – I was channeling Alice.

'Sure, I have time owing, a lot actually. Where are we going?' I asked, excitement bubbling inside me.

'I thought you could take me shopping, then I could take you shopping and we could try a few different dining experiences and see a few sites, like tourists, which we are...'

I sat grinning at him like an idiot. 'That would be great. But men don't like shopping, you'll be bored after an hour.'

'I'll be with you and watching you, and I could do that all day,' he said. 'We can do some tourist stuff too, huh? You haven't asked where I've booked it.'

'Where?' I asked.

'New York, the city. Is that okay?'

'New York City,' I squealed, 'hell yeah, that's fantastic. There's so many good sites and so much good shopping there – I have to do some research... there's this amazing haberdashery store in Harlem, and great shops in Brooklyn and Williamsburg, plus there's really good vintage markets...' I noticed Nik grinning at me and I hugged him, knocking him back on his back.

'I heard there was a very good Victoria's Secrets store there too,' he teased. 'I have to take you there.'

'I'll add it to the list but we're guy shopping first!' I clapped my hands. 'Thank you, Nik, that will be so much fun,' I said, kissing him all over.

He laughed and looked so pleased to have pleased me.

'How are we getting there?' I stopped to ask.

'Well it's about five-and-a-half hours flying time, but we lose a few hours in time difference so if we leave early Friday we'll be there late afternoon, just in time to check-in, take a walk through Central Park because I'm dying to see it together, go for a drink, and go out for dinner later. Then Saturday is all yours... you will have to plan it... I'll need plenty of coffee I suspect... and Sunday we'll fly home after midday but we get the time difference back so we'll get home mid-afternoon. Okay?'

'More than okay, brilliant,' I said, still squealing.

'We fly from the local airport here direct. Early start.'

'I'm good with early,' I assured him. 'This is so exciting. I have to do some shopping research. What will I wear?' I could hardly sit still.

Nik grabbed me closer. 'Before you fly away planning this adventure, I have to tell you something,' he said, seriously.

'Sure.' I settled down and looked at him.

'I know I was a bit out of it at the hospital, Sah-sha, but I meant what I said to you.' He watched me and drew a long breath. 'I love you, I am in love with you, and I promise you, my past can't hurt us,' he said. Before I could respond he pulled me towards him and kissed me as though he needed me.

Chapter 18

I woke up so happy and it was hard to get to work on time with Nik trying to pull me back into bed all the time – he was taking full advantage of not having any training this morning. It was extremely unfair and selfish – I would have to put that on his performance report. I had to banish him to the kitchen while I showered and even then he kept sneaking in to watch my silhouette in the smoky shower frame.

I heard him groan and the next minute he was in with me.

'Nik, I'm going to be late.' I playfully hit his arm as he curled his body around me.

'But this will get you fired up for the day,' he offered helpfully. His hands began to wander over me.

'Not fair,' I moaned and between waves of pleasure, I studied my German man; he looked pretty damn sexy wet. I pulled away, dropped to my knees in my huge shower and caught him by surprise. He leaned back against the wall and muttered a few encouraging German words – at least I think they were encouraging because I'd heard them before a few times when I was doing something similar.

My shower was perfect for two – I designed it to be sexy but I didn't realize just how perfect it would be. Score one for me, or Nik pretty soon. I gave it to him all in one package and fast: women are great at multi-skilling. I could hear his breath hitching and within minutes he was pulling me up and closer.

'I don't think I had any control,' he said between breaths. He looked at me as though I had just conquered him.

I grinned like a champion. 'That's the idea, buddy – I've got to get to work and I like to leave my man happy.'

'I've just been worked over,' he said with a smile, breathing out. He began to reciprocate and I blocked him with the soap – I had some good moves of my own.

'I'm more of a mid-morning, lunch, afternoon, night person,' I said, 'but you can make me very happy if you make me coffee and raisin toast while I dress.'

'Are you sure?' he asked, before moving his hand down my body. In no time I heard the satisfied groans coming from my own throat – my body was just doing its own thing.

He released me. 'Not even a little bit of a morning person?' he asked but didn't wait for an answer. Instead he whirled me around to face the shower wall and began working on me, pressing his body against me. I took only a few minutes more than Nik did to give into it, water beating down on me as he slipped his hands around parts of my body.

He held me until I stopped shuddering and then he lightly smacked my butt.

'Hurry up or you're going to be late. I'll get that raisin toast packed to go.' He walked out of the shower and I watched him towel dry – great ass, great back, such solid legs, beautiful shoulders – and then he put his track pants and T-shirt back on and disappeared to the kitchen. Yep, I think I might be a morning person after all.

*****

We moved our usual beer and burger night at the local hotel from Wednesday night to Thursday night because Max and Ren had a family thing on the Wednesday night – Ren's mom's birthday – but they still wanted to catch up. It was lovely how accepting Ren's family was of Max, Ren's mom loved him. It helped that Max did her hair too.

'You know Thursday is not beer and burger night,' Ethan said, drily. 'It's pots and pasta night. But luckily, I'm good with that.'

'Me too,' I agreed.

'I'm still having a wine regardless,' Max said. 'My turn to order,' he said, and taking our money and orders, headed to the counter with Ren on hand to help out.

'How's Nik?' Ethan asked. 'Tell me he's still on the scene please?'

I studied my sweet, older brother who looked so worried for me. Bless him.

'He's on the scene and it's great, surprisingly great,' I said, and he grinned, pleased.

'No really great,' I said again. 'I went from not interested to trying to avoid him and now to right in amongst it so to speak... that's not good is it?'

Ethan bit his lip and shrugged. 'There's no rule book but maybe this time, just don't marry him in three months like last time. I'm not saying you wouldn't have made your marriage work, but living with Adam first probably would have shown you he's not so good at 'until death do we part'.'

I nodded. 'You got that right. Can I ask you something before Maxie and Ren return?'

'Sure,' he said, and leaned forward. He looked particularly handsome tonight in a navy hoodie, white T-shirt underneath and pale jeans – a bit sailorish.

'You know Nik's an orphan and Anton more or less confirmed that Nik was abused by one of his foster parents...'

Ethan nodded, keeping up.

'He said something strange to me last night,' I said, lowering my voice. 'I touched his scars and he said "I promise my past can't hurt us", or something like that. What does that mean? Should I be worried?'

Ethan frowned as he thought about the words. 'Well, like I said, there's no manual for this stuff, but I'm guessing it could be one of two things. He is being hunted by a hitman or the mafia and he's over here getting away from them and while you're both here, he's feeling safer...'

I grimaced at my brother. 'What's your second suggestion and let's hope it is better.'

'Abandoned or abused children often think they're not worthy of love, in their mind that's why they've been abandoned. Nik's experienced it twice – his own parents didn't want him so he was fostered out, then he had a foster parent who abuses him. Kids can think they're at fault. So I'm just having a shot in the dark here, but Nik's learned from all this—'

'—learned not to trust?' I interrupted to ask.

'Not necessarily,' Ethan continued. 'He could have learned some positive things like who to trust and how to cope with trauma, but his view of how stable and safe the world is, is probably shot.'

'Interesting you should say that because when he woke from the concussion and was a bit disorientated, he asked Anton were they safe,' I said.

Ethan nodded, thinking about that. 'In terms of what he said to you, that his past can't hurt the two of you – traumatic experiences can cause someone to think things will go wrong at a moment's notice and that there's a risk getting close, but he's saying he'll take that risk if you do. Or, he may think that he's worked hard now – he's successful and got financial stability so he's not undesirable like he was as a kid, in his mind anyway. It's hard to know. But, often kids from adversity also work hard to do something valuable with their lives. He's doing that.'

I exhaled. 'Wow, makes you realize how really good we had it. How do I get it right so I make him feel safe?' I asked Ethan.

'Same way you would anyone else,' he said. 'Love him, tell him that, be supportive, be kind, be positive with your praise.' Then Ethan read me well, like he always did, he could see right through me.

'Sassy, don't over think this or think it is a burden, just go out with the man he is now. You like him, you love him?'

I raised my eyebrows, sort of confirming both.

'Then live in the now as he's asking you to do.'

Chapter 19

I was at the front door waiting for Nik to pick me up in a taxi on Friday morning at six-thirty when he messaged to say he was one minute away. I was convinced we were going to miss the plane... we might have only had to go a short distance to the airport but we were cutting it fine for a seven-fifteen takeoff.

Jim was happy for me to take the day off, as the club didn't like staff getting to much leave accumulated. Kay took the day off too which meant poor Alice would have the whole area to herself or maybe that was a good thing. She was green with envy – I like to shop but Alice loved to shop and she was good at it, so she helped me with my Saturday New York City shopping list. I don't think Nik had realized what he got himself into.

I saw the taxi coming down the street and it pulled up beside me. Nik jumped out, gave me a kiss and grabbed my bag, pushing it into the trunk as the taxi driver held it open.

'You look gorgeous,' he said, and gave my black felt hat a tug. I was just wearing jeans, black high heel boots, a white button-down shirt and black jacket but it pleased Nik. I glanced towards the taxi trunk with our bags in it and noticed Nik had brought a small overnight bag for himself and a suitcase.

'Wow, you've traveled heavy,' I said. He had more luggage than me.

'The suitcase is empty Süsse,' he teased. 'I thought you were serious about this shopping exercise?' He opened the taxi's back door and I slid into the seat and moved over as Nik got in beside me.

'You think of everything,' I said, admiring him.

'I hope so,' he said. He leaned over to kiss me and tasted of toothpaste and smelled of soap and fresh cologne. 'Morning,' he said, as he pulled away.

'Morning, my guy. I'm so excited I couldn't sleep. I hope we won't miss the plane.' I shuffled on the seat with excitement.

'We won't miss the plane,' he promised. He was clearly more relaxed than I was about catching planes. The driver took off quickly – I suspected he was worried he'd have a freaking-out female in the back seat if we were late.

Nik reached for my hand and engulfed it with his large one. I was so excited to have the day off and be going away for a weekend, looking at fabrics, shopping for Nik, sightseeing, being with Nik. Sigh, it doesn't get any better does it?

'Got the tickets?' I asked as the thought occurred to me.

He nodded. 'We don't need passports before you ask.'

I gave him a smirk, but it had crossed my mind.

'Where are we staying?' I asked.

'I booked The Pierre on E 61 Street. Anton said it has a very good view of Central Park and a very good bathroom,' he said, suggestively. 'I hope it will be all right.'

'We're going to New York City together for a long weekend; the youth hostel would have been fine,' I assured him, squeezing his hand with excitement. Seriously I was like a school kid on an excursion!

The airport was in sight and instead of going to the domestic departures, our taxi driver followed a different road and several minutes later we stopped in front of a charter area. I looked from the driver to Nik and back.

'Thank you,' Nik said, and gave the driver the fare and a tip. Before I could ask any questions they were both out of the car and I followed. Nik put my bag and his small bag into the one empty suitcase, and we thanked the driver again, moving out of the way as he departed. Nik headed towards a gated entrance.

I stopped. 'Where's the plane?'

'There,' Nik said, nodding towards a small plane.

'You've chartered us a plane?' I said, my eyes huge.

'It's the quickest way to get there, it'll save us time,' Nik said, so matter-of-factly that I laughed. He took two steps back to where I stood rooted on the spot, took my hand and led me along. 'Come on, you don't want to miss it, remember?'

I think my mouth was open and I snapped it shut once I realized.

'You've chartered us a flight to New York?' I said, again,

hustling to keep up with his long strides even if he did have my hand.

'Sure, it'll be fun,' he answered.

I'm not sure what happened then because I think I was in a mild state of shock, but in less than fifteen minutes we were ushered into the gorgeous plane interior, we met the captain and were given the safety demo. Our luggage was stored, I was sitting back on a big white leather chair and looking at Nik opposite me, his legs wrapped around mine.

'I told you we wouldn't miss it,' he said, with the hint of a smile.

'Nik, this is amazing, it's too much,' I said. We began to taxi for take-off.

'Too much what?' Nik asked, with a frown.

'We're spending your money dining out, now flying and staying the weekend in New York. I don't want to send you broke.'

Nik grinned. 'I think I'll be okay.'

'Seriously,' I continued. 'You know money isn't a big deal to me but I'm the daughter of a developer, you need to invest and not throw away money on me on meals and weekends away and chartered planes...' I was raving now.

Nik held up his hand in a stop motion and then he took mine. He went to speak but we began take-off and we stopped to watch the plane rising and the ground disappearing below us. When we were stable, and the captain removed the seatbelt sign, Nik moved over to sit next to me.

'Sah-sha, I don't want you worrying about money, but

I appreciate it. Anton is my financial adviser, and I'm an accountant, so we have it all worked out. I have several residential properties and a couple of commercial properties rented out in Germany; I have stocks and shares, and my expenses here are very low... I pay next to nothing living with Cassie and Alice. I can spend a bit of money having a good time. I'm investing in you,' he said.

'But what if it is not a good investment or you want your money back?' I asked.

'It's a great investment and I've already had more in returns than I dreamed off. I'm here with you,' he looked at me intensely. 'I want you to relax about this now Sah-sha, think of it as spending some of the bank's interest on my account. I've pre-paid everything I could for this trip, I have a card ready for us to go shopping and I'm cashed up. No more talk of it, just fun. Ja?'

God this man was gorgeous.

He pulled me . 'Agreed?' he said again, and I nodded.

'Good,' he said, and then we kissed. A wonderful romantic, long, wet, tongue kiss that left me weak. When he released my lips, he pulled me onto his lap to straddle him.

'I've never flown like this before,' I said, wide-eyed with surprise.

'I hope not,' he said, pushing against me. 'We have our own supplies,' he said, with a glance to the small kitchen-bar area. 'So there'll be no interruptions, no flight attendants,' Nik said and slipped off my jacket. 'I know you're not big on morning sex...'

'Oh I am,' I assured him. 'I just said that yesterday to throw you off track so I could get to work on time.'

'A very good strategy that didn't work,' Nik said recalling our shower episode. He began to undo the buttons on my white shirt revealing my white lace bra and I think he just got harder if that was possible.

'Sah-sha, so beautiful,' he said trailing his fingers over the lace. He continued to study me until I distracted him by undoing his belt and unzipping his jeans. I worked them slightly down his hips; he cooperated fully lifting us both slightly... truly remarkable how that weight training can come in useful.

He wriggled to get a condom out of his jeans pocket and I took it from him, released him from his white boxers – very hot too may I say – and slipped the condom on. I rose slightly, slipped my jeans down and re-straddled him. He made a very impressive guttural sound in his throat.

Then I slipped down onto him. His hands grabbed my hips, moving me into place slowly. He pulled away from me long enough to look at me and murmur my name. Then I gave him some movement. His hand gripped the back of my neck and I rocked on him, watching as his jaw locked and he closed his eyes, feeling me around him. His breathing increased and so did mine – what a great way to start the day. Being in control of the lap dance, I moved to get him in just the right place, applying just the right friction. My hand shot out to his shoulders and my nails dug into him. I called out his name, or I think I did... I might have called out 'God, yes,' as well.

Nik read my movements and moved me faster, controlling my hips. We both came in uncontrolled pleasure – my back arching, and Nik burying his face in my chest. I felt his body shuddering, I love that. We breathed heavily, finding each other's mouths and kissing between breaths.

I drew back and eventually I dropped my chin onto his head as he wrapped his arms around me tightly, pressing his cheek against my chest.

'I love you, Sarsh. I am truly happy,' he said.

I couldn't stop the tears welling in my eyes. I wanted to protect him, to give him everything and make the rest of his life so happy. I pulled away, blinked my eyes clear and looked at him. He smiled a slow, sexy smile and I bit my lip.

'Ich liebe dich,' I said, to him and his eyes lit up and then he laughed. I playfully hit him. 'What? I've been practicing with the online translator.'

'It was perfect Süsse, perfect,' he said, smiling and studying me.

'Really?' I asked, narrowing my eyes.

'Absolutely! Thank you. Now I need to get rid of this condom and you need to cover yourself,' he said.

He lifted me off him and I adjusted my clothing and I watched as Nik did the same.

'Can we make a coffee?' I asked, studying the kitchen.

'I imagine so,' Nik said, disappearing into the small bathroom. He resurfaced and found me in the kitchenette with two cups, coffee, a percolator, milk, cream, boxed cereal, fresh fruit, fresh muffins and more.

'Look what I found! I'm always hungry after sex and we haven't had breakfast.' I eyed off the muffins.

'Speaking of food, I was thinking we could meet Anton and his girlfriend for dinner Saturday night if that was okay with you? We need to have dinner tonight just the two of us. What do you think?' he asked.

'Sure, that would be fun,' I agreed. 'Have you met his girlfriend?'

Nik shook his head in the negative. 'She's a local and I think you would call her an extro...'

'Extrovert,' I helped.

'Yes that's what Anton says. He's fairly quiet, so she might be good for him,' Nik said.

I carried our coffees back to the chair and came back for a muffin. Nik selected several boxes of cereal and was making a mix.

'I want to walk through Central Park this afternoon together after we check in to the hotel. Okay? It's in walking distance,' Nik said.

'Sure. Then, let's have a bath together and drink champagne. Does it have a bath?' I asked.

'Of course, it was a prerequisite to my search. I know you are particular about your bathroom, and it has a beautiful one.' Nik joined me again on the big white leather chairs. We were awake now and full of questions and plans. 'Have you got your shopping destinations sorted for tomorrow?'

'Absolutely,' I assured him, 'but I'm not telling you in advance in case I freak you out,' I said.

'Did you put Victoria's Secrets on the list?' he asked.

I rolled my eyes. 'Yes Süsse,' I copied him, making him laugh again.

'Good. Then as long as I get to wake up with you, make love to you and see you try on underwear, nothing will freak me out.'

I fanned myself. I should have had a cold drink.

Remember how I mentioned we were jinxed? Well plans have a way of changing.

Chapter 20

When we landed, Nik had a car waiting for us – must be that accountant's brain, so organized – and even though we gained three hours on the clock, we arrived at the hotel and were checked in by late afternoon, still plenty of time for a wander through Central Park. Oh and the hotel... breathtakingly amazing. I hoped Nik and I had time to 'christen' every room because it was the most beautiful hotel I had ever seen. When we put the key card in the room, our single piece of luggage was already there, but I ran around the rooms like a kid in a candy shop.

'It's huge,' I said, my eyes wide as I raced from the suite's living area with its classic cream, gold and timber furniture, to the bedroom with the huge bed that we could lose ourselves in later tonight, and then I saw the master bathroom as it was called – wow. I ran my hand over the black marble of the deep bathing tub, oh yeah, we would use that. Nik watched me from the door, his arms folded, a grin on his face. I ran back over to him and leaped at him, and he caught me in a hug.

'It's so amazing,' I squealed, 'but we didn't need a suite, it's huge.'

'I know, but I wanted a room with a view of Central Park,' he said, and carried me to the windows where we could see the park framed by the city skyline. 'Look at that!'

'This is so amazing,' I continued to rave.

'You are,' he agreed, kissed me and put me down. 'Let's go for a walk through the park, come on.'

I raced to change into my lower-heeled boots and grabbed a hat for Nik which he didn't know I had bought him – a classic wool black porkpie hat. I put on my black hat and presented it to him. He laughed as I reached up and placed it on his head, he looked adorable – like a member of a ska band.

'Perfect, suits you.' I grinned at him, admiring his form in his jeans, black boots, long-sleeve black and white shirt and now a very well-appointed hat. 'Got the key?' I asked at the door.

He flashed it at me.

'Phone, wallet?' I asked. He gave me a look that implied I was a bit anal and I shrugged. 'I like my checklists.'

He patted each pocket to indicate he had both and held the door open for me. We caught the elevator down and wandered through the beautiful lobby, out into the streets of New York City – I know, so cool – and to the park. It was amazing, Nik was right. It was like this oasis in the middle of a frantic city... quiet, peaceful and soul-restoring. I looked up at Nik as he strolled beside me holding my hand, looking adorable and I couldn't remember ever being so happy. I thought I had been granted my happiness quota with Adam, but this was right, this was better and I was being given a second chance.

'Let's get a popsicle,' I said, seeing the van.

Nik smiled. 'Wow, I haven't had one for years.'

'Me either.' I selected a green frozen popsicle with a red stripe... something about a rocket on the wrapper. Nik had an ice-cream. He was probably starving since the last thing he'd eaten had been cereal hours before.

We sat on a bench, watching the lake and licking our popsicle and ice cream. I flashed my tongue at Nik.

'Is it green?' I asked.

He laughed, leaned down and kissed me, then sucked on my tongue.

'Very green, froggy,' he said, pulling away from me. 'Want a lick of mine?'

'Always,' I said, 'oh you mean the ice-cream, no thanks I'm good.'

Nik shook his head at me. We finished and wandered around until I found the Alice statue. I took a photo of it and sent it to Alice.

She messaged back right away calling me a 'lucky duck' and saying she was just leaving work now – Jim had given her an early mark. I forgot work was going on somewhere in the real world. Then Nik got a message from The Russian and burst out laughing. He read it out.

'He and Lucas said there was going to be a meeting when I got back. First the girls want to learn to tango after Tomás performed at the lunch, now the girls want to be taken shopping in New York,' he said, with a grin.

I read over his shoulder and The Russian had put in capitals, 'IT HAS TO STOP'.

'I'll tell him to lift his game with the girls.' I nudged Nik. 'You've raised the bar.'

He smiled, shrugged, pocketed the phone and took my hand again. 'Want to try out our bath with champagne?'

'Hell yes,' I said, and increased our walking speed.

'Are you going to be able to wind down enough tonight to sleep?' Nik looked at me suspiciously.

'Depends how exhausted I am,' I said.

'Got it,' Nik said, hatching plans.

*****

Nik took the room service wine list away from me. 'I'll order, you go run the bath,' he ordered me.

'Why, don't you trust me to select?' I asked, a bit offended but kind of happy not to have to pick, as everything was so expensive.

'No. You'll try to save me money and order something horrible,' he said. 'Bath.' He nodded to the deep tub waiting to be filled. I obediently smiled and turned to go. I heard him on the telephone moments later ordering a bottle of Bollinger. I didn't know much about champagne, but I knew that was good, very good.

Not long after that we sat surrounded by bubbles... sipping our champagne in the bath. The city skyline view was visible from our deep bath but with enough of a screen to give us privacy. Nik massaged my foot. I heard his phone ping with a text message.

'Someone's after you,' I said, sipping my champagne.

'Don't care. You have such cute little feet.'

'They're not little,' I assured him, 'they're just little compared to yours.'

'Mine have to hold me up. Where shall we go for dinner?'

'I thought you would have that sorted?' I gave him a surprised look.

'I've booked a place for eight,' he said with a glance to the clock. It was seven o'clock. 'But I didn't want to dictate if you had somewhere you would like to go.'

'If you trust me with the shopping, I trust you with the eating,' I told him. 'Where are we going?'

'Anton has picked for tomorrow night, but I went online and found the top ten restaurants in New York City voted by the public and found one a few streets from here – it's French. Okay?'

'C'est excellent!' I said, attempting some French.

Nik grinned. 'Do you speak a little French?'

'Nope,' I assured him. 'Thank you my guy, for all of this. It has been such a huge surprise and so much fun,' I said, holding his gaze. He colored slightly, not using to being thanked, I think.

'Thank you Süsse for coming with me.'

'There would be girls lined up for miles to come with you,' I reminded him, putting down my champagne.

'But you're the only girl I want to come with me,' he said

and grabbing my legs, he slid me towards him, placed his hand on my cheek and leaned in to kiss me. His hand moved to behind my neck as he cupped me and tasted me. He pulled away and I felt in the water, finding his erection.

'Can this wait until tonight?' I asked. 'Because I want to play for a long time later.'

'I can wait but you had better remove your hand,' he warned. 'I love that I get to have you tonight and have you all night.'

'Just don't wear yourself out completely,' I threatened him. 'I have a big day planned tomorrow sightseeing and shopping for you.'

'And shopping for you,' he reminded me, 'we're doing both. Right?'

'Right,' I agreed.

'I mean it,' he said.

'I know, but we're starting with you,' I said.

He nodded. 'We'll wrap that up in an hour or so and then, I want to see you trying on outfits for me. We should get you a new dress to wear tomorrow night to dinner.'

I shook my head. He was too perfect and I was a goner. His phone beeped again.

'You had better check it in case it's a family emergency,' I said, the words slipping from my tongue before I realized what I said. My eyes widened. It was such a normal thing to say. 'I'm sorry, I mean perhaps Anton is trying to—'

He held up his hand. 'It's okay.' He reached to the floor for his jeans and pulled his phone out of the pocket. He thumbed to the message and laughed. 'You won't believe this?' he said, and held the phone up for me to see. It was a picture of the two of us on a bench in Central Park. We were wearing our hats and eating our cold treats. I had my tongue stuck out and Nik was laughing.

My eyes widened. 'Someone spotted you; we were sprung!'

'Apparently. It's online, my manager just sent it to me; cute photo,' Nik said.

'It's our first photo together,' I said, romantically, 'even if my tongue is out.'

'I'm partial to your tongue.' Nik glanced at my mouth. 'I'm going to get my manager to buy two copies of the shot from the photographer and send it to me – one for both of us. Ja?'

'Ja, great thanks.' I waited until he messaged back. 'So who is your manager? You rarely call him by his name.'

Nik put the phone down. 'I only met him when I came here late last year; he's a nice guy, James Moffat, in his forties or so, married, two teenage kids... that's all I know. Anton recommended him.'

'Does he live in Santa Ana?' I asked.

'No, he lives in Los Angeles but he visits and we have lunch once a month to go over stuff. He's with an international company and they assign the nearest agent to the sports person, so in my case, it's James.'

'Are you his only Saint?' I asked.

'I am, but he's got other soccer guys, a few baseball players, female tennis players, and basketball guys,' Nik explained. 'He looks after anything related to my contract, sponsorships, requests, management fees, whatever.'

'Maybe I should get a manager,' I teased.

Nik gave me a slow smile. 'I'm happy to take on the responsibility of managing your sexual satisfaction.'

I raised an eyebrow in his direction. 'It's a very important job,' I said.

'Not one I'd take lightly,' he said, and began to prove it. I pulled away and he groaned.

'May I remind you Niklas that we said we would wait until we got home later to work that big bed and we have a dinner appointment in less than thirty minutes? You need to lead by example and get out of the bath,' I bossed him.

Muttering a few German words and looking like he'd been banished, Nik sighed and agreed, then pulled himself out of the bath. Magnificent view. I just loved it how well he followed orders, most of the time.

*****

We walked to the restaurant which was good for our appetites, and fortunately I had selected heels I could do a marathon in. We weren't big eaters, just particular eaters... although Nik could consume a fair bit of food with his size. We were placed in a window seat and I hoped we weren't going to see our photo on some online social site tomorrow. Nik checked I had underwear on before he ordered – his logic was that if I tempted him, he wasn't going to be trapped having to feed me first like last time. Lucky for me I wore panties and a matching bra.

The French food was good, a bit rich but I had taste buds

more tolerant of that than Nik. We decided we would skip dessert – I know, almost unheard of for me, but the entree and main were so delicate and I was kind of keen to get home to bed... and not to sleep. I snuggled under Nik's arm on the way home, as we took in the atmosphere and window-shopped.

'I'm giving that restaurant seven-and-a-half out of ten,' he said.

I looked up at him. 'Wow, that's tough. I was thinking eight-and-a-half.'

'It was too fussy, too many sauces.' He shook his head.

'Yeah, well there was no sauerkraut on the menu,' I teased him and he got me in a pretend headlock and mussed my hair.

'Very funny, Sah-sha,' he said, releasing me and I grinned up at him while attempting to fix my hair which was messy by nature anyway. We entered the lobby of our plush hotel and took the elevator to our floor. When we entered our beautiful suite, Nik slipped his suit jacket off and disappeared into one of the bathrooms and I went into the other. He came out smelling of fresh mint and fresh skin... just right for licking.

He stopped when he saw me; I had brought some new lingerie for tonight and I was hoping it would get his attention. It was an unlined baby doll set with matching panties in soft lilac, very short, and at the back it had a deep plunge back with a satin crisscross bow.

'Wow,' Nik said, and breathed in deeply. Just the reaction I was hoping for. His lips twitched in a smile and I did a full turn for him. 'I get to unwrap that bow,' he said with a look that was part lust, part longing. He didn't take his eyes off me as I lingered near the bed; he slipped off his shoes and socks, undid his belt and slipped off his coat pants. Oh my indeed... nothing like a tall, blond man in fitted white boxer briefs. He hesitated for a moment then slipped his shirt off, revealing his naked and tanned chest, scars, ink and all... superb.

He moved towards me, sat himself on the end of the bed and reaching out for me with those long, toned arms, he pulled me between his legs. It took all my restraint not to knock him back on the bed, pull those briefs off and take him – my self-control is incredible.

Nik trailed his fingers over the fabric of my lingerie. 'Magnificent, Sah-sha, you are the most beautiful woman I have ever seen.'

I think I flushed three shades of red, as I've never been called beautiful. I've been called lots of flattering things, but even Adam-the-ex never said I was beautiful.

Nik slightly lifted my baby doll skirt to admire the matching lace panties and with a grin, turned me around and undid the satin bow. He turned me back around to face him and gradually slipped it off until I was standing in front of him in only see-through lilac panties. Then, he growled and licked me. I squealed with his tongue tickling me and he picked me up, turned me around and placed me on the bed... and he kept licking and laughing as I reacted to his tongue. I watched him, this beautiful man, teasing me, laughing, fuck I loved him, fuck I was hopeless.

'Are you okay?' He stopped and looked at me.

'Uh-huh,' I nodded, leaning up on my elbows. 'Why?'

'You stopped breathing,' he said, matter-of-factly, 'relax, breathe.'

'Breathe, right,' I said, and fell back flat on the bed. I heard him chuckle.

'Now this is a dessert I would give ten out of ten for,' he said.

His warm breath teased me and I arched and moaned, wriggled and got in trouble for wriggling – it wasn't fair of him to be so good.

Then the weirdest thing happened, I started to get emotional – knowing this was Nik touching me, this wonderful man who had made me so happy and made me feel so safe, that tears flowed down my face as I moaned with pleasure. I restrained from screaming as I came – as much as I wanted to – my body clenched, my muscles drew so tight that I wish he was in me to feel it. He moved up the bed to hold me, embracing me while I came down and trust me that took a while.

'Sah-sha!' His eyes widened with alarm and he raised my head to look at him. He wiped tears off my cheek. 'Did I hurt you?' he asked.

I shook my head. 'No, not all. I just love that the man I love is so good at making love to me. I'm a crybaby.'

He visibly relaxed and smiled. 'You are beautiful, my Süsse.'

'But now, I want you,' I said, getting my lust for him back in focus. I pushed him off his side and onto his back and ordered him up the bed. I sat on his legs and ran my fingers over him; truly breathtaking how good he looked tonight and how hot his body was.

'I've never, ever seen such a body,' I said, returning the favor. He reached for me but I had a better idea. 'Nik, I want you to lie back, behave and leave this to me.'

He grinned. 'Not sure I can leave it entirely to you, Sarsh.'

'On the contrary, you're very good at following orders – there's a lot to be said for conscription.' I moved up to sit on him and he warned me.

'You're playing with fire there,' he said, with a hitched breath, 'besides conscription has been abolished now.'

'Not in this bedroom buddy,' I said. 'I want you to think of me as your commanding officer – Major Sasha.'

Nik laughed. 'Uh oh,' he said, and looked a bit apprehensive.

'Trust me?' I said. This was not just an exercise in fun sex, he had to trust me to see his scars without being self-conscious or trying to reach for his T-shirt.

He hesitated. 'Okay,' he nodded.

I returned to kissing him, long, wet, seductive kissing. I wanted him as badly as he wanted me; I just loved seeing and touching every inch of him.

I returned the favor making love to him and he came with a passionate roar, his whole body strained. He pulled me tight against him as he continued to power inside me. His face was buried in my neck and his grip on me was so tight that I swear he was never going to let me go.

Eventually, his body relaxed into mine and he stroked my hair. We fell back onto the pillows.

I was in his arms and in heaven.

*****

In the early hours of the morning, my hand reached out for him – Nik was moaning, talking and groaning in his sleep. I looked to the clock, five a.m., and still so dark outside. He tossed suddenly and said something in German. He called out again and his body began to shudder. He repeated a few words in German.

'Nik,' I said, trying to stir him without completely waking him. I placed my hand on his chest and his eyes shot open, his chest rattled with a large gasp of air and he reeled back from me, staring as though he didn't know me. He glanced around trying to get his bearings. He was shaking and then his eyes focused on me.

'Sah-sha,' he panted, and sat up.

'It's okay, you're safe,' I said, using Anton's words from earlier.

He balanced his elbows on his knees, the sheet pooling around him, and rocked slightly. 'Fuck,' he muttered again, his fingers massaging his temples.

I sat up next to him, placing my hand on his back and he flinched with my touch. He was still breathing way too fast.

'I'm sorry I woke you,' he panted. He ran his tongue over his lower lip and then ran his hands over his face.

'What were you seeing?' I asked, and he shook his head.

I stroked his back for a few more minutes and then I lay back down and, grabbing his arm, I pulled him towards me. I directed his head to my chest and he allowed me to hold him. I stroked him, his hair and back, until his breathing returned to normal and his body stilled and that's how we stayed.

I think my Nik, my strong man, needed help for some of those skeletons in his closet. An hour later, he rose and whispered he was going for a run. I imagined him running around Central Park in the pre-dawn light getting the demons out of his head, as I lay alone in bed missing him.

Chapter 21

I heard Nik return from his run and hit the shower. Ten minutes later he crawled back into bed beside me, naked and smelling fresh. He spooned me, wrapped his arms around me and inhaled.

'Mm, you smell delicious and warm,' he said, snuggling up to me.

I gripped his strong arms, loving the feel of him against me.

'Are you okay?' I asked.

'I am,' he said, and said no more.

'Does running help?' I asked, pushing him a little to open up.

I felt him hesitate before answering. 'It expels a lot of stress.'

'You could talk to me, I won't be horrified, you won't put me off you,' I told him. Again he said nothing. I continued: 'It might help... you know, sharing and trusting me.'

'I trust you Sarsh, I just... I know how to deal with it myself. It's nothing, don't worry about it,' he said, and shut me down.

I felt kind of pissed off, like I had been dismissed. I got that he didn't want to talk about it, but he was happy to ask me a hundred questions about my family, my divorce and to let me be open and trust him.

He started to move, to touch me and the feel of his hands teasingly rising under my tank top sent tingles all over me. I pushed his hand away.

'I've already come. I know how to deal with it when I need it, don't worry about it,' I said, quoting his words back at him. Was that childish? Give a fuck, this works both ways.

He pulled away and pulled me over on my back to look at him. I couldn't work out from his expression if he was angry, bewildered or both.

He studied me, breathed out a deep sigh and then his jaw locked. I returned the favor, holding his gaze, giving him a pouty, locked jaw look too. Mine was better than his I think. Eventually he spoke.

'Sarsh, I don't know what to tell you... there's some things I want to keep from you but that doesn't mean I don't trust you,' he said.

'There's things I want to keep from you too, Nik,' I said. He looked a little surprised. Using one of my brother's counseling expressions, I threw it at Nik. 'How does that make you feel?'

He frowned. 'I guess a bit suspicious, a bit worried that you feel you can't share stuff with me.'

'But you might not like me if you know everything,' I said, continuing to use his logic.

He made a scoffing sound. 'Nothing you could tell me

would make that happen.' He pulled me even closer to him. 'I know what you're doing Sah-sha. If you think I don't trust you, then you are wrong.' He ran his fingers through my hair as he stared into my eyes. 'If you think I don't want you to know me, that's not true either. I just... I just don't want you to see me that way.'

'What? Brave, a survivor, a fighter, tender, sensitive, sharing?' I asked.

He shrugged.

'Please, tell me a little about your childhood Nik,' I said. I lay side-on, resting on my arm and he turned onto his back and exhaled. Clearly he didn't want to, and I waited, watching him. I could almost hear his thoughts ticking over so I started him.

'Did your parents die?' I asked.

He gave a small, shake of the head. I didn't push that angle.

'But you were in the foster care system or was it an orphanage?'

'Foster care. A lot of foster care.'

'Why?'

He shrugged. 'Sometimes people can take a few kids, sometimes things change and they have to give them back. Other times it was only ever meant to be temporary but if you're lucky, you get a good foster family and can stay with them for a long time.'

He wasn't making eye contact with me, just staring at the ceiling. I placed my hand on his chest and stroked him.

'Did you have a good family?' I continued to lead him.

'Not until my coach took me in. I was a bit rebellious for a while, so I got ditched a lot. Then I learned to keep a low profile and stayed in the same place for a few years. Then another kid and I scored a couple who started out okay but it turned out bad,' he said.

'Is that where you got the scars?' I said, running a finger over some of them. Nik flinched as I touched a few.

'I think they were happy when they took us in, but she had an affair. You don't understand that as a kid, but when I think back now on their fights, I think that's what it was about.' He began to accept my affection and leaned up to put his arm under me, pulling me against his chest. 'They started fighting a lot and Joachim – that's the other kid they fostered – we just tried to stay below the radar. I was twelve then, Jo was about nine.'

'What happened? Did they stay together?' I asked.

'No. He started beating her, she started drinking, staying out more, having the affair. He started hitting us as well, and eventually they came to remove us. I don't know what happened to Joachim, never saw him again. But that's when my first coach and his wife took me in – Sebastian and Britta. They were in their thirties and had no kids, I don't know why, I didn't ask. But that was the best thing to ever happen to me... I stayed with them from thirteen until I was twenty.'

I smiled, seeing him smile. 'Do you stay in touch with them?'

'Sure. My room is still there. Anytime I'm home, Britta insists I stay there and Seb calls me the day after every game to analyze the game. He's a very good coach and mentor. I got lucky.'

'So how did these happen?' I asked, touching his scars again. 'Did your foster father do more than just hit you?'

Nik signed; he seemed to be resigned to telling me now. 'Some nights he needed somewhere to put his cigarette out,' Nik said, and I gasped. 'See, this is why I don't want to tell you these things, you'll get upset.'

'I am upset, but I'd be more upset not knowing you. And these?' I asked, looking at a series of small scars.

'Just from stitches,' he said.

'From stitches!'

'A few cuts and hits, that's all.' He stopped.

'Didn't you tell someone? Didn't Anton notice, or your teachers?' I asked, raising my chin from his chest to question him.

'I made Anton promise not to tell,' he said.

'Why?'

Nik shrugged. 'I didn't want anyone to know.'

'It wasn't your fault,' I said.

'Süsse, when you're a kid in foster care, everything is your fault. Adults aren't wrong.'

I drew a deep breath, taking in all the awful images I had of a young, blond boy being mistreated and in pain, and alone. 'How did they find out or did they separate first and then you were removed?' I asked.

'They took Jo and me away after I was hospitalized.'

I gasped again.

'My "foster-father" went a bit too far with his fists and

broke a rib or two and knocked me unconscious. Then they took us both out of that house.'

I couldn't believe the words that were coming from his mouth.

'Nik, it's so awful. How can any adult do that?' I said. 'It's a weird world – you have my parents who undertook a dozen IVF cycles to have us and yet there are people who can just push kids out of the womb and they're not fit to be parents. I wish my family could have rescued you and adopted you.'

He grinned. 'I'm glad they didn't. We would have been like stepbrother and stepsister which would make this very awkward.'

'True,' I said, thinking about that technicality. 'So, do you have any happy childhood memories?'

'Of course,' he said, a little defensively.

'Tell me one to cheer me up,' I said.

'You tell me one first,' he said, deflecting again.

'Okay,' I thought. 'Our house was always a bit crazy, not always in a good way. Mom and Dad both worked, there were five kids and we weren't that close as kids, not like we are now. Saffy and I were close of course but having three older brothers meant you had to compete for everything. They destroyed everything we owned and teased us a lot too.'

'Is that why you like living alone?' Nik asked.

I looked up at him. 'I don't know, I hadn't thought of it in that context before, but maybe. I think my happiest memories were the holidays. We were always camping or caravanning, fishing, swimming, learning to surf or paddle. We spent most of our holidays busy and outdoors and Mom and Dad took time off work and spent it with us. Those were the best times.'

Nik nodded and looked at the ceiling as he thought.

'I think the best time for me ever was when I was thirteen and I went to live with Seb and Britta. I'll never forget when they showed me through to the room that would be mine,' he grinned and looked at me. 'It was the first time I ever had something that was mine – my own room, my own bed, a desk, a chair, a cupboard and some clothes in it. I kept waiting for it to disappear.'

I ran my hand gently over his chest as he spoke. I couldn't imagine it. I always shared a room with Saffy, but that was different. I still had plenty, I was given so much and here was Nik waiting for it all to vanish.

He took a deep breath and continued. 'For the first few months, I would wake at night and get up. I'd touch the desk and chair, check in the closet and if everything was still there, I'd go back to bed. It's a bit embarrassing now, but one time Britta removed some of my things to wash them and she found me crying in the corner of the room. I thought she was packing my things for me to go.'

Tears welled in my eyes as he told me the story. Such a different world from everything I had ever known.

'After that, she would always tell me it was washing day… for years after.'

We sat in silence for a while until he rolled off his back, pushed me on mine and edged up my top.

'Did you really do it without me?' he asked.

'Are you kidding? Of course not. Why would I self-serve when I have the master on hand?' I teased him.

Nik smiled and nudged my top up all the way. We became just a little closer from shared relations on several levels.

Chapter 22

It was his own fault, all his own doing – any man who takes a woman shopping is asking for trouble and I worked him. Not once did he complain but I don't think he'll shop again for some time, maybe a year, maybe more. We got Nik new jeans, dress pants, shirts, pullovers, T-shirts, shorts, socks, jocks... yeah, I was a big help there, and even shoes. I got him a couple more hats too because he had a good head for them. His credit card got a workout. Then, true to form, he took me shopping starting with a trip to Victoria's Secrets.

I laughed when he asked: 'can we buy those white angel wings there?'

I gave him a strange look.

'You know,' he insisted, 'like they wear in the fashion parade. I want to sit in a chair at the end of your catwalk and watch you walk towards me in lingerie with angel wings.' He took a deep breath.

I moved in front of him just accidentally brushing against his jeans where he was sporting a sizeable bulge as he imagined the catwalk scene. It was an accident, honest. Nik groaned and pulled me closer.

'You better stay there for a few minutes,' he suggested.

Seriously, hopeless! 'We don't have time to wait or hide all day,' I whispered in his ear and brushed against him again with a smile.

'You're not helping the situation, Sah-sha,' he said, and narrowed his eyes at me suspiciously. I gave him my best innocent look again. Eventually we were able to leave with three new lingerie purchases; it would have been more but I restricted Nik and his super-quick credit card reflexes to just the three. He was way too keen to spend money on me, awful that.

We were fueled by several rounds of coffee during the morning to sustain Nik and after a very successful shop, we stopped for lunch. Next, we dropped our shopping back to the hotel and went sightseeing for the afternoon. We got back to the hotel in plenty of time for another stroll around Central Park before dusk and another long soak in the tub – we needed it after the day's effort. I also had a new dress for tonight for dinner with Anton and his girlfriend.

*****

When we arrived at the restaurant called *Terraces of Manhattan* – Anton's choice – he was there already with his girlfriend, who took me by surprise and delight. She was dressed in a very risqué fashion even by my standards. I was in my new dress that Nik had brought me – a stylish wrap-around with very high heels to accompany it. I hadn't got a matching hat yet, but I would. Nik wore one of his new button-down shirts with dress pants and looked good enough to be on the menu. Anton was conservatively dressed but his girlfriend was in a bright red dress and just in it!

'Nik, Sasha, this is Amanda,' he introduced her, after shaking Nik's hand and kissing me on the cheek.

'Mandy,' she said, shaking our hands enthusiastically, 'everyone calls me Mandy.'

Anton was bookish, slender, even nerdy but handsome in a boy-next-door way, but his girlfriend was a true *Noo-Yorker* all the way to the accent. She was a big girl, with flowing red hair down her back – I know, red dresses on redheads, hmm the jury is out on that one. She had a sizeable bust that I couldn't take my eyes off so I had to forgive Nik for staring, and she was more sassy than I was a Sasha, if you get me. She had lovely green eyes and was full of confidence and energy.

If opposites attract, then Anton and Mandy were made for each other. She had enough personality for all of us and I felt instantly at ease with her.

'I love this place,' she gushed, 'it's my new favorite, but I have a different favorite every week don't I babe?'

Babe nodded. 'She does,' Anton agreed, looking at her with adoring eyes. I began to relax, this was going to be an easy dinner, I wouldn't get a word in and wouldn't have to do anything but nod and smile... too easy. Unfortunately that didn't quite work out so well for Nik – yep, it appears Mandy has no boundaries which was kind of good for me.

We were seated at a table for four near the window with a view to the busy street; inside the restaurant however, everything was calm and beautifully lit.

'You have to try the lobster; it is a real dining experience and the chef, Marcus, he is a genius,' she said.

'What else would you suggest? I'm not a lobster girl,' I asked her.

Mandy was up to the challenge providing plenty of other suggestions. Nik and Anton were talking between themselves while we girls scanned the menu.

'The grilled sashimi,' she gushed, 'to die for.'

'I can taste it already,' I said, teasing her. I closed the menu. After we ordered wine and entrees, Mandy dived straight in.

'So Nik, Anton tells me you grew up together but you're an orphan. Have you ever tried to find your family?'

I nearly fell off my chair and Nik choked on a sip of water. Anton looked embarrassed but not shocked – clearly, he was used to Mandy. It was definitely going to be a weekend of getting to know Nik even if that wasn't his plan.

She continued, 'I only ask because one of my friends searched for her parents and found them and now they are one big happy family... well her mother anyway, her father died not long after they were reunited.' She stopped for breath.

Well this was good – I had been wanting to ask this too but I was doing the cautious thing as my brother Ethan suggested... tip-toeing around the subject, finding out bits and pieces and not pushing topics he clearly didn't want to cover and this was one of them. It was so out of character for me as a journalist and way too direct for my own good, but now Mandy just blew all of my prep work out of the water.

'Well.' Nik cleared his throat. 'A few years ago I did look into it.'

Anton tried to change the subject as the drink waiter brought out wine, but Mandy wasn't having it. If looks could kill, then the look Nik was giving Anton would have had him on life support.

'So, did you find out anything?' she said, brushing Anton's arm affectionately. I sat there in stunned silence, my eyes wide, not sure if I should rescue Nik or wait for his answer... I really wanted to hear his answer. Nik gave Anton a look that was a bit hard to read but it had a rescue-tinge about it. We clinked glasses in a toast to good health and after a sip, Nik continued.

'Well I found my biological mother – she told me she was sixteen when she got pregnant with me to an older man and they were never going to be a couple. Now, she is married with a family, but she doesn't want to rekindle anything... she was scared I would wreck her new home life. Her husband didn't know her past,' Nik said. 'She sent a Christmas card this year.' He shrugged.

'And your father?' Mandy asked.

Nik glanced to me – I couldn't read his expression – then he looked back to Mandy.

I could see Anton was dying – whether he expected Nik to kill him later or he was truly sorry for throwing Nik in the deep end I couldn't tell.

'She gave me his name but she said he never knew about me, she didn't tell him and she's had no contact since that night. Her parents were strict and sent her away to a relative's place until after the birth and they organized my fostering.'

I reached out and took Nik's hand and changed the subject. It wasn't our business to know all this personal stuff and I didn't want him to be put in the spotlight... he looked so uncomfortable.

'We went shopping today,' I said brightly, way too brightly. 'Nik survived.'

'Oh my God, did you got to Tate Alley?' Mandy asked and began gushing about the shoes there.

Nik squeezed my leg under the table and gave me a grateful look. I kept Mandy occupied on our shopping adventures and the conversation did not return to Nik's childhood again. Phew. But I wanted to know now if he had tried to contact his father. Must have been heartbreaking to contact his mother and have her still disinterested – to think she had no idea of the years of abuse that he endured. I wanted to shake her, but I guess she was young and frightened to find herself pregnant. My heart ached for Nik.

Mandy was right about one thing, the meals were divine even if I found it hard to eat without wanting to put something in Nik's mouth. His hand coming and going from my leg did nothing to help the situation. Before coffee arrived – believe it or not, I declined dessert again – I excused myself to go to the bathroom.

'I'll come too,' Mandy said. 'We have to go together... girl rule,' she told the boys.

'Absolutely,' I agreed, even though I could see Anton giving me a look that said *don't leave me, you know he's going to kill me...* what could I do? He was right though, Nik was cheesed off. I glanced back before heading into the ladies and could see Anton talking himself out of it and Nik had a serious jaw lock action going. Anton probably should have been more discreet but I don't totally blame him – Mandy was one of those people who put herself so completely out there that you found yourself talking to her. I think I just told her my star sign and my fantasy to ride naked, bareback on a very dark horse, down the beach in summer – yeah, don't ask.

When we returned there was coolness in the air even though the boys were making small talk about mutual friends. I slid into the seat next to Nik, took his strong jaw in my hand and kissed him. His eyes softened and his jaw relaxed. See, I was good for him. Something else seemed to get harder too but that was just inconvenient.

Mandy oohed-and-aahed as dessert arrived for her and Anton. Nik and I were just on the coffees. I love a woman who appreciates her food and she did, every mouthful got rated.

'I'll pick up the check tonight,' Anton said. 'I'm just glad we got a chance to catch-up before you head back.'

Nik went to protest. I guess he was used to paying and was probably super aware he was financially worth ten times more than all of us.

Anton held up his hand. 'I want to; it was my invitation,' he said.

'Thank you, Anton, that's very generous, and it was a great choice,' I said.

'It's a pleasure, and yes, Mandy knows her restaurants,' he said, with a smile towards her. 'Besides, I'll eventually charge

Nik for it somehow... you know, slip it onto his account,' he said, with a wry grin towards Nik.

'So that lunch you picked up the last visit?' Nik asked, his lips twitching in a smile.

'Yeah, the pleasure was all yours,' Anton teased him, and Nik smiled and shook his head. Looks like we were all friends again, phew.

No sooner had we said goodbye to Anton and Mandy, and left the restaurant, than Nik pulled me to a stop and wrapped his arms around me.

'I'm sorry about that stuff at dinner,' he said.

I frowned at him. 'I don't understand why you are apologizing to me,' I said, studying his face. I touched his cheek. 'I'm sorry if it embarrassed you or put you on the spot.'

'It threw me, I have to be honest,' he said.

I took his hand and we started walking back to our hotel.

'Will you finish the story? You don't have to, but did you contact your real father?' I asked.

He pulled me under his arm and we walked on. 'I tracked him down. He was about ten years older than my mother so I don't know how they got in that situation but it sounds like a one-night stand.'

'Who would have thought something so perfect could come from that,' I said, looking up at him.

He grinned and squeezed me tighter.

'I wrote him a letter... old fashioned I know, but emailing didn't seem to cut it and I couldn't call him out of the blue.' He swallowed. 'It's been a year and I haven't sent it yet.'

'Nik!' I exclaimed, looking up at him. Then I remembered what Ethan said, play it cautiously. 'Why not?'

He shrugged. 'Sometimes it's better to not know than to be... unwanted.'

'I understand, I think. But what if he is excited? He doesn't even know he has a son. What if that is great news. Would it be for you if you found out you had a son?'

'I've tried to put myself in that situation several times. I think I'd be pleased. What about you?' he asked me.

I thought about it. 'It's so hard to say – a woman will always know if she has a child in the world.'

Nik grinned. 'Yes, I guess so.'

We came to our hotel for our last night in New York City and entered, greeting the night staff as we made our way to the elevators.

'Do you think I should send it?' he asked.

'It's entirely up to you... but yes, I do. What's the worst that could happen? You find out who your father is and score yourself some family. If he doesn't want to bond, you carry on like now, nothing lost, nothing gained. Trust me, family is good to have sometimes.'

The elevator came and we entered and kissed all the way to our floor. The elevator doors opened and we exited.

'Send it. I'm here for you no matter what happens,' I told him, as he scooped me up and carried me into our room like we were crossing the threshold on our last NYC night.

'Thanks Sarsh, I told you that stuff couldn't hurt us and I don't want you to think it is a problem.'

'Nik, I don't see it as a problem, not for a moment, and there's nothing about your past that could hurt me,' I said.

I spoke too soon.

Chapter 23

As we strapped into our large leather seats on the chartered plane to return home, Nik's phone beeped with an incoming text message; we forgot about it while we talked about our trip and the highlights. Nik reminded me that he loved me and I reminded him I felt the same.

'It was the most exciting trip, ever,' I gushed. 'Thank you, Nik.'

'The pleasure was all mine Süsse, all mine,' Nik said, graciously. 'Wait until we do Paris and London, and I take you home to Berlin!'

His legs encased mine and he leaned forward during takeoff; we held hands watching New York City disappear beneath us. Once we could undo our seatbelts, I moved over to sit next to him and we just held each other. We slipped down to lie along the length of the seats, spooned together, and he stroked my hair. I must have fallen asleep because I woke as I felt the plane preparing for descent. Nik had been sleeping too. We were pretty exhausted from our nocturnal activities amongst other things.

We sat up and I attempted to straighten everything that was now crooked. The light came on to buckle up and we put our seatbelts on again. I reminded Nik about the text message he had received and he reached for his phone, thumbed the screen and read the message. His face went ashen. He swallowed.

'What is it?' I asked.

'It's from James, my manager,' he said, frowning. He looked a little stricken, his lips thinned and his jaw locked.

'Are you okay?' I asked.

He looked up at me as if he had forgotten I was there, and he pocketed the phone. He glanced out the plane window.

'Nik, you can tell me. What's wrong?' I asked. My stomach started to swirl with anxiety.

He closed his eyes momentarily, then opened them and leaned forward.

'Sarsh, something bad has come up and it's not true, and I love you.'

I felt the blood rush from my face. It wasn't fair. Please don't let me be hearing this.

Nik took my hand. He didn't look well and he avoided my eyes.

'Just tell me,' I whispered, 'Nik...'

He licked his lower lip again and looked at me. 'There's a story in the paper about a model who says she's expecting a child to a Saints' player.'

'A Saints' player... it's you?' I said, and the words sounded strangled coming from my suddenly dry throat. I couldn't swallow.

'It's not my child, Sarsh, she's saying it is, but I promise, it is not my child.' He undid his seatbelt and leaned forward, taking both of my hands in his. 'Sometimes women say those things to trap a guy, you know, to look after them... to get alimony from someone they know can afford it, but it's not my child.'

I could barely hear him; I went into some sort of shock. I had just had the best weekend of my life with a man I loved, a man who I decided to trust and now I was going to lose him, now he was having a child with someone else. I think he said something, but I couldn't hear him for the rush of thoughts in my mind.

I interrupted him. 'Do you know her? Did you have sex with her?'

'Yes,' he said, honestly. 'But since the moment I started with you Sah-sha, I promise I haven't slept with anyone or seen anyone, not a single woman, you can trust me on that.'

I nodded. 'How pregnant is she?'

Nik lowered his head and reached for his phone. I noticed his hand was shaking slightly – he was as anxious as I was. He opened the press clipping on his phone – it was a shot of her modeling, a glamor shot – I reached for his phone and he gave it to me; I read the article. She was claiming to have a child with Nik but she didn't say how far along she was, she was coy and had just said first trimester. It may have been Nik's if she was far enough along. We mightn't have been together then but this changed everything.

'She's beautiful, you would suit each other,' I said, my voice choking.

Nik grabbed the phone from me. 'You're beautiful, you suit me, you fit me, Sah-sha.'

We began our descent and Nik was in panic mode.

I told him to put his seatbelt on but he ignored me. I reached over and did it up. I was always practical even when my stomach was swirling. He tried to take my hand but I pulled away, I didn't need the influence of his touch on my skin – I needed a clear head.

My actions only stressed him more; he ran his hands through his hair, his leg tapped and both of our thoughts filled the small confines of the plane. The moment we touched down – while we waited to exit the plane – Nik called his manager and listened as James explained what had broken out in social media.

Why do people get off on this crap? Why would she want this kind of fame? Why are the media interested?

I heard Nik insisting James take it to a lawyer and demand that she get a paternity test. He hung up and dropped on his knees in front of my chair, grasping my hands. He raised my chin so that I would look him in the eye.

'Sah-sha, please believe me, it is not my child. If it was, I would provide all the support in the world for that kid, but it wouldn't change what we have, I love you, and I want to be with you.'

I nodded again. It was all I could manage. I had to be alone to process this – our perfect weekend, my future as it was shaping, it all looked different now. Aagh, everyone at work would know! Why did I date a player? why did I let him into my life? I dug my phone out – I had put it away earlier for the flight – and it beeped too with a missed message and call from Alice about the story. Nik's phone began to go wild with texts and calls coming in and he put it on silent. He stood as the hatch door opened. We alighted and took the car that Nik had waiting for us. It was only early afternoon because we had gained a few hours. We drove home in silence, Nik not letting me move away from him.

I turned to him in the taxi and put my hand on his face. He was super distressed.

'I need to be alone now, to think,' I said. He started to protest and I placed my fingers across his lips. 'Just leave this with me. You go do what you need to do.' I kissed him and as the taxi pulled over out the front of my apartment, I got out and took the suitcase the taxi driver retrieved for me. I stopped Nik from bringing it upstairs, and insisted he got back in the taxi. I hurried in before any photos could be taken of us arriving home should anyone be loitering with a camera. I entered to find Prada waiting for me – Saffron had fed him for me – I was so happy to see him and to be in the safe surroundings of my home. I was alone, again.

*****

Over the next few hours I had calls from everyone I had ever known – all my family, Ethan and Saffy several times, Alice, my parents, Maxie, even a phone message from Anton, but I let them all go to message bank. I had to return to work tomorrow and I just needed to work through the pain and stress of this situation.

About seven o'clock there was a knock at the door and I decided not to answer until I saw it was Nik outside. I let him in. He pulled me to him, desperate and in pain. I clung to him too.

'I'm so sorry about this Sah-sha, but it's not my child, I'll prove it to you. I have never cheated on you, I promise, I wouldn't,' he insisted, stroking my back.

'I believe you wouldn't cheat, Nik, I honestly believe you,' I assured him, touching his face as he pinned me against the wall near the door. We hadn't got much further than the entrance. 'But we don't know how far along she is, it could still be your child?'

'How? I've always worn a condom, like we do. Always.'

'It could have broken,' I said.

'It didn't break. It was one night and it didn't break. She's fallen pregnant and she's done a rough calculation, but it isn't me,' he said.

I offered him a coffee or drink but he declined. We were both sick with heartache. I couldn't eat or drink for the pain.

'Nik, I have to tell you what I'm thinking,' I said. We stayed against the wall holding each other. 'I think we need to take a break.'

'No Sah-sha, don't do this,' he begged me. 'Don't do this.'

'Shh, hear me out. This woman might have just been a one night stand, but you're going to share something. If it is your child, you're going to see her grow with your child and you're going to be there when that child is born – all the time the two of you sharing this experience. She's beautiful, it is only natural you'll be attracted to her throughout this.'

He shook his head and I quietened him so I could finish. I continued, 'You'll wonder should you give the child a family – a normal life, should you both give it a try. You of all people know how important that is. All the time I'll be somewhere in the background, in your way.'

'No Sarsh, don't do this.' He shook his head.

'You know deep down inside I'm right. And I love you Nik,' my voice broke as I said it, 'but I can't bear to think of you bringing a child into the world and sharing that experience with someone who is not me. If you already had kids that would be different, but this is an experience I'm not going to be part of. We need to separate until you sort it out, if you sort it out.'

'There's ways we can manage this. I've been thinking...' he started, but I shut him down.

'At the end of the season, Nik, I'm going to go away... go and live in Paris for six months and design and work. I need to get away – there's so many memories here that I have to have some distance from them until I get perspective.'

He buried his face in my hair and breathed deeply.

'I love you Süsse, this changes nothing for me. Please stay with me, we'll sort it out.'

I pulled away and shook my head. He studied me with a direct gaze and then he righted himself, pulled me closer again and kissed me. Releasing me and without looking back, he headed out the door and I locked it behind him. I was sick to the core.

Chapter 24

I was cried out by the morning and a little tougher with the shock warn off. I was ready to put on a brave face and I did just that. I headed into work.

'What's happening with you and the Kaiser?' The Russian asked on seeing me. I felt Alice and Kay look over at me – they had asked was I okay but avoided questioning me given I looked so morose. I took a deep breath and turned my attention to The Russian.

'Off limit discussions today Russian include Nik, New York City, shots of me with my tongue out, Nik, anything that is not work-related and Nik,' I said, in my best commanding voice.

He strode towards his office and muttered, 'Well that's just boring isn't it?'

I couldn't help but smile and I saw Alice trying not to. The Russian was persistent though, and I knew that wouldn't be the end of it. Kay braved the subject.

'Are you okay, Sasha?' she asked in a quiet voice.

I looked at her and shook my head in the negative. I

couldn't speak and she and Alice understood. Kay nodded.

'We're here for you darling,' she said, which just brought tears to my eyes which I quickly blinked away. I whispered my thanks, it was all I could get out; I turned my focus to the computer and began to field the emails of media requests I had, ignoring the ones related to Nik's pending child.

He had called me this morning but I didn't answer. His message was desperate and I didn't know what to send him back. I just wanted to work and try and get back into that space I had been in pre-Nik, it had been a good space, I had been happy and focussed. Today, I just wanted to go under the radar. I returned messages to family and friends to say I was okay and going below ground. The day passed slowly as I tried to avoid contact with the world and just work. Nik respected my wishes and didn't come into the office.

Ethan didn't give up that easily and neither did Max. They both came around to my place that night with wine and therapy. Later that night when I was alone Alice called to tell me that Nik had a bad time at training... all the guys thought he was a legend and a stud or plain unlucky to get hooked. Men... they really were from a different planet. She said Nik was a mixture of despondent, angry and defeated – he had gone to his room, hadn't eaten and hadn't surfaced since. I told Alice there was nothing I could do about it. I lay on the bed and my phone rang, again. It was Nik. I answered.

'Nik—'

'—I miss you,' he said, cutting me off.

'I miss you.'

'Can I come around?' he asked.

'No.'

'Are you okay Sarsh?'

'No.'

'She says that she is eight weeks. It was just before we met… so… I have to wait two weeks to get the paternity test done, when she's ten weeks,' he said. 'They can't do it earlier. I've got James and a lawyer working on it. The club just thinks it's a huge joke.'

'They're not doing anything to help protect you?' I asked, surprised.

'No. I guess they think it's my mess.' He sighed.

'So you've spoken with her?'

'Yes.'

'How did you get her number?'

There was silence. 'I had it,' he said, reluctantly.

'So, it was more than a one-night stand?'

'No, but she put her number in my phone before she left. I've never called her or wanted to,' he said.

'Just sex?'

He took a deep breath, treading carefully. 'She was a nice girl that I met out one night after a game. I don't think either of us planned on anything more than a night in bed.'

'She's beautiful and she's going to always be the mother of your child, forever,' my throat thickened and my voice choked. 'You'll have so many firsts with her, and I wanted you all to myself. I wanted us to have a few firsts.'

'Well, getting married won't be one, but it will be our first time together,' he reminded me. I was a bit taken aback, Nik wasn't the nasty type but maybe he was starting to get angry with my attitude.

'No, sorry, I guess you can't be my first husband, but you could probably have that with her,' I retorted. He made a fair point though. It was not the time to retaliate with another line; it was time to stop, step out of this and not make a bigger mess of it than it was.

'There's nothing more to be said really, Nik. We can't do this for another two weeks while we wait, and then who knows, you might have another life.'

'Sarsh, we can do this, I'm not the father, I know.'

'I don't.'

There was silence again.

'I can't be without you,' he said.

'And I can't be with you. So please don't say that to me.' I felt the pain in my chest at his words. 'Please don't contact me Nik. Just go, sort this out, leave me alone now.' I hung up.

I hated thinking of him talking to her about their night together and now their pending child. I wasn't a drama junkie, I didn't need the pain. I just wanted to lick my wounds, stay in and lie low. Soon it would all go away. I know, I remembered the pain from Adam, and it went away. It always goes away if you wait long enough.

*****

I didn't sleep, I didn't eat, I drank too much wine. I really had to pull myself together. I arrived at work looking like a zombie. Good thing Jim didn't notice; he was blissfully unaware of the emotions of his female staff most of the time. At least I could keep busy. I had a game this weekend to prepare for, a media release to be done, stats to gather and interviews to organize.

The Russian stuck his head out of his office and asked me to come in.

I rolled my eyes. 'Not talking about it, Russian,' I said, with a glance to the window. Where was the goddamn coffee van when you needed it?

'It's a security matter, Sash, I need to talk with you,' he growled and disappeared back into his office.

I rose, accepted a sympathetic glance from Kay and Alice and headed his way.

'Close the door,' he said, as I entered. I closed the door and dropped into Ed's seat; he wasn't in yet. The Russian was wearing a suit today.

'You're looking a bit spiffy, what's going on?' I asked.

'Could say the same about you,' he returned the compliment to my pin-striped suit. 'But then again, you usually dress up. I've got some client meetings,' he explained.

I nodded. 'What's up?' I took a deep breath, waiting for the Nik discussion which I didn't need. I was so raw, every mention of him just cut me more.

'Where are you at with Nik?' he asked, directly.

I frowned at The Russian. 'Why do you need to know?'

'I want to know what support he is getting and where he's at in his head. Lucas, Shayne, the club in general, they're not taking this very seriously but we should be providing some kind of media security or support for our players.'

I looked at The Russian with surprise. 'That's very understanding of you Russian. But I assure you I have the media side of it locked down. It's a no comment situation and they're not getting to talk with Nik about it.'

'Good.' The Russian sighed. 'There was an incident last night that I'm trying to keep under wraps.'

I bit my lip, I had been worried about some fallout. 'What happened?' I asked.

'Bloody Buzz, biggest mouth on the team, I swear that guy has fuel in his blood he's so aggressive.' The Russian shook his head. 'He made some smartass comment to Nik in the parking lot after training asking if it was the most expensive fuck he's ever had.'

I groaned. 'What happened then?'

'Nik went him. Absolutely fucking full-on. It took me, Lucas and Jackson to pull him off.'

I began to chew my nail. 'How's Nik?'

'He came out okay. Buzz is black-and-blue, going to say he ran into a door, a couple of times – and maybe fell down the stairs – that's the unofficial line since no-one knows except you, me, Lucas and Jackson.'

I shook my head and swore under my breath.

'Sash, he needs someone to lean on,' The Russian said.

'He's got someone; she's expecting his child,' I said, and I left his office.

Chapter 25

Alice put down the phone, grabbed her keys and handbag and rose to leave the office.

'Where are you going?' I asked.

'That was Shayne. He asked me to come around to his office and bring my home keys,' she said, with a shrug.

I watched her walk off and wondered what the hell that was about. Alice lived with Nik, I had heard from Nik that morning and he had been alive and kicking so... had he locked himself in his room? Were they running a drug test on him? Were they looking to borrow an outfit from Alice? So many questions so little time. I pushed it to the back of my mind as the phone rang and I had one of the journos on the line wanting to speak with a player for a weekend interview. Sigh. Douglas from the local suburban paper called every week and the paper had a readership of about two – Douglas's dad and cousin. Yet every week I had to 'waste' a player on an interview with him. It was so hard to get the players to do media as it was, and I hated to use up my favors. I told him I'd get back to him ASAP. I tried asking for the questions hoping I could do it that way and peddle the answers to a few outlets, but he was onto me.

Thirty minutes later, Shayne called me on my office extension and asked me to come around to his office. Mm, this was getting interesting. I told Kay and Jim where I was going and passed Alice in the hallway returning to her desk.

'What's happening?' I asked her.

'It's about Nik,' she said, and lowered her voice. 'He's gone AWOL.'

'For fuck sake,' I muttered and wandered around to Shayne's office, knocked and entered an ambush. *What the fuck?*

Shayne was sitting down, Captain Lucas was pacing and The Russian was standing with his arms folded blocking the window... well almost.

'Hi Sash, close the door,' Shayne said.

'What's going on?' I looked at them suspiciously.

'Nik's bolted,' Lucas said, and stopped pacing long enough to look at me and for me to notice how particularly handsome he was in his British way. 'We're hoping you can help.'

'Define bolted,' I said, narrowing my eyes.

'Packed and left,' The Russian added.

'What? He's got a two-year contract,' I said, 'hasn't he?'

Shayne nodded. 'I think we might have let him down,' he said, with a sheepish glance to The Russian. Makes me wonder if The Russian had some experience in this and knew how Nik was feeling. Shayne continued, 'We need to fix this before we lose him for good and the media get a hold of him leaving, breach of contract, all that drama.'

I dropped down into a seat in front of Shayne's desk.

'We didn't take him seriously,' Lucas said, 'the girl getting pregnant, it was all just a bit of a laugh but it obviously wasn't to Nik and we blew him off.'

'Sasha, we need you to call him,' The Russian said.

I shook my head. 'My private life is just that, Russian. If you guys want to fix it with Nik, then you call him.'

'We've tried,' Shayne said.

'What if we called him on your phone Sasha, but we'll do the talking?' Lucas asked.

'He'll answer,' The Russian said. 'We need to do this before he goes back home to his family and friends.'

'Sash,' Shayne called for my attention, 'as Lucas said, we've kind of dropped the ball with Nik and we need to fix this.'

I looked from one to the other. 'You didn't tell them Nik has no family?' I asked Shayne. 'I know you like to keep things private, but this is one time when he could have used the club's support.'

Lucas and The Russian looked at me with confused expressions. 'Shayne told me Nik's next of kin was his financial adviser, Anton, who is his childhood friend. That's all the family he has.'

'Fuck,' Lucas swore, 'that makes it worse. We really blew him off, no-one helped him and we let the media vultures get him.'

'Thanks,' I said, being one of those.

'Sorry,' Lucas acknowledged, 'I just meant we didn't realize this was such a big deal to him and we should have been looking out for him.'

'We should have had a protection order around him,' Shayne said.

I nodded. 'When this is over Shayne, you and I better sit down and write an issues management strategy... what the club does in the event of a number of scenarios like this to protect the players and the club – you know for club in-house fighting, drug issues, bad press, all that stuff,' I said. Shayne agreed.

'So will you talk with him?' The Russian asked me.

As intimidating as the three guys were, it was none of their business.

'No. What Nik and I do isn't the club's business. I'm not going to go out with a guy who's having a baby with a groupie model just so you can keep your asset,' I said.

'No one's suggesting that for a moment, Sash,' Shayne said, 'but we accept we've handled this badly and I guess we're just asking you to help us fix it from our end and... maybe, try to support him until the paternity test is done? If it's negative, will you two get back together, assuming it is all over? Have you discussed that?'

I didn't know if he'd have me back given I had run away from the whole situation, but I'd have him back in a heartbeat, because I did believe it had happened before I'd been on the scene and I... well, I loved him, damn it. But I didn't need him, a new baby, a connection with this other woman hanging over us – we didn't have enough history to sustain that and I didn't want the drama. Besides, he should have the chance to make a new family without me in the way. What a mess.

'If it was all cleaned up, if it wasn't his kid, yes,' I said, honestly. I lifted my phone, found Nik's number, thumbed it and handed it to Lucas. He put it on speaker and pressed the call button. I didn't think Nik was going to answer and then after five rings he picked up. He took a deep breath and said my name.

'Sah-sha?'

'Nik, don't hang up, it's Lucas,' the captain said, leaning forward to speak into the phone lying on Shayne's desk. 'I'm with Shayne, Russian and Sasha. Where are you?' Lucas asked.

Again with the silence. Lucas looked up at Shayne and The Russian.

'Nik, it's Shayne. You've taken your gear from Alice's place, but I need you to come in and have a chat. We can work through any issues you have with the club... where are you?'

'I'm at the airport,' Nik said.

The three guys looked at each and The Russian puffed his cheeks out with concern. I bit my lip, this wasn't good. Was he going home to Berlin?

'Buddy, I'll come and get you,' Lucas said.

'No. I came and saw both of you. What's to say now?' Nik almost snarled the words. For a guy who had been through so much he had always been so up; it was bizarre to hear anger in his voice.

Lucas was looking at the ceiling. I could hear his mind working overtime as he tried to decide how best to handle this. He moved around to sit next to me and took a large breath. Leaning into the phone reception, he continued, 'We handled this badly Kaiser, I'm sorry. I should have taken it more seriously instead of blowing it off as a joke.'

Nik spoke. 'Luke, if some girl came out in the media and said she was having your child and your girlfriend Mia walked away, how funny would you find that?'

'Fucking not funny at all,' Lucas said, bristling at the thought.

'The club should have stepped in and stepped up, Nik, we missed this one, I'm sorry,' Shayne agreed with Lucas. 'We want to fix this and we'll fix it so it won't be handled like this ever again.'

'If that kid was mine, I'd take full responsibility,' Nik said, 'but it's not, the paternity test will show that. But you know, all that aside, I've had enough.'

The men looked at me and I shook my head. I didn't know what to say, I had nothing.

'I spoke with your manager, James, this morning,' Shayne said. 'I've told him we've got our solicitor working on it—'

'—I have my own solicitor on it. I don't need yours,' Nik cut him off.

Shayne swallowed. 'Even so, James has put your solicitor in touch with the club's solicitor and we'll manage this now. We'll get the tests and we'll shut this down.'

'You know why I came to the Saints?' Nik asked. He didn't wait for an answer. 'I had six international offers, big offers, all the same. When I met with you, Luke, you said you wanted to play with the Saints because you were near your friends. The money wasn't the main priority. You talked about the importance of club loyalty, sticking together, the club looking out for each other. Fuck that was just bullshit.'

'No Nik—' Lucas started and Nik cut him off.

'—the Saints are just like every other club. Just play well and give us our money's worth. That's all that matters,' he said. 'And you know what, that's okay, I was not being realistic.'

'Nik, I promise you, you are wrong. I fucked up, the club fucked up, but you're important to us and the club as well. I don't want you to leave. I'm coming to get you and we'll fix this,' Lucas ordered stepping into Captain mode.

There was a silence on the end of the line again.

'Where exactly are you at the airport?' Shayne asked. There was a silence again.

'Kaiser, don't make me get my airport security buddies to take you in for a strip search,' The Russian threatened and broke the tension. I think I even heard Nik scoff.

'The departure lounge. My flight leaves in an hour,' Nik said.

The Russian spoke. 'Give me the flight number and I'll get my buddies there to pull your bags off.'

Nik hesitated and then gave his flight number.

'Okay, this is what we are going to do,' Shayne said. 'Nik, has anyone spoken to you? A journo?'

'No. I've signed a few fan autographs and been in some photos,' Nik said.

'Right, I want you to head to the arrivals and sit there. You're waiting to collect a friend, that's why you are in arrivals. Lucas is on his way, stay there until he arrives and calls you and then head out and he'll pick you up. Leave your bags, we'll get them sent to the club. Yes?' Shayne said.

'Will you come Sah-sha?' Nik asked.

'Yes,' I said.

'Stay put buddy, we're on our way,' Lucas said, and hung up. We all breathed a sigh of relief.

'Let's go,' Lucas said.

Shayne held up his car keys. 'You'll need more than two seats,' he reminded Lucas.

'All that money spent on a car and you can't drive around more than two people,' I shook my head and Lucas smirked at me. Might as well get a few shots in while I can.

*****

Lucas and I hardly said a word on the way to the airport. Normally I would have been super consciously aware of sitting next to one of the sexiest and biggest names in soccer, or I would have been pushing him to do more media for me, but I was too busy stressing out about seeing my own sexy guy, Nik. Thank God Nik didn't go home – I know I had told him to leave me, but I hadn't been thinking straight. I guess I thought if, when, he sorted it out and got the DNA results back, if he wasn't the dad we could pick up again. I didn't think he'd leave the country and I might never see him again. I felt chilled at the thought.

Lucas didn't call Nik on our arrival. Instead, I asked him to park and to let me go in and meet him. Lucas thought it was a good idea and pulled into the short-term parking. He said he'd return a few calls while he waited. I left him and rushed into the arrivals area. I spotted Nik straight away –

246

sitting low in the chair, watching the airplanes through the glass windows, his long legs out in front of him. My heart stopped momentarily... just seeing him caused me pain and desire. I took a deep breath, moved up behind him and draped my arms around his neck.

'If that's Luke, it's taking friendship too far,' he said.

I stuck my tongue in his ear and he groaned and grabbed me from behind, pulling me forward onto his lap. I cupped his face in my hands and I watched as his eyes looked wet. He blinked.

'Glare,' he said, explaining it.

'Don't go,' I said, 'I love you.' I don't know where that came from, from the heart I think. I hadn't planned on saying it but I meant it.

He pulled me tight to him and kissed me deeply. 'I love you, Süsse. I want to marry you, and travel the world with you... I'll do soccer commentary and you can design in every city in the world that inspires you and we'll have beautiful children, and a handsome dog and Prada...'

I laughed. 'Can you just come back first?'

'Okay,' he agreed.

'I can't believe you were going to leave.' I held him. 'Why? Where were you going to go?'

'I needed to go back and spend some time with Seb and Britta. They would put my head straight,' he said. 'Besides, you were going to clear out, to Paris.'

'Not anymore,' I said, shutting him down. 'I'm sorry Nik, I just had no manual to handle what happened.'

'Me either,' he said. We stared at each other and he smiled, the tension falling off us in waves.

'I was so busy being lost in my own pain, I didn't have room to contemplate yours,' I said, stroking his face.

'It's okay, I understand,' he assured me, holding my gaze.

'C'mon, Lucas is waiting in the car. You gave them a scare, they all feel very bad now,' I told him.

'How do you feel?' he asked me seriously.

'I'm still scared,' I said, softly.

He nodded. 'We'll be okay, no matter what, we'll always be okay as long as we stay together. We're a team.' He extended his hand. I shook it.

'Team Wagner and Saxon,' I said.

Chapter 26

A text message woke me the next morning and then another. Nik's phone started about the same time.

'What the—?' I rolled over but Nik stopped me.

'Kiss me first,' he said, reaching for me. 'Last time we got all those messages it wasn't good news. I want to kiss you first in case you throw me out again.'

I smiled at the gorgeous man lying beside me. God it was good to have him back in my bed. I know nothing had really changed – he might still be having this baby with another woman but we weren't good at handling it apart, best we handle it together. Besides, I've read lots of fairy tales, so I guess I could be a good ugly stepmother.

Nik's hands ran over me and then held me tight before he placed a soft morning kiss on my lips.

'Thank God you are back with me Sarsh,' he mumbled.

'It was great sex last night,' I agreed, with a smile and he gave my butt a tap.

'Smartass, but you have a cute one,' he said.

We looked at each and then taking a deep breath, I

reached for my phone. Nik did the same. I sat up quickly – this was good, great, fucking brilliant news. Nik gasped beside me, put the phone down and slid down, back into bed. He didn't move, I think the relief was just washing over him.

She had been caught out. There was a huge story on her in the paper – a basketball player from San Francisco had come out and said she tried the same thing on him. He was married and had a fling with her. She had faked being pregnant to extort money from him in return for disappearing from his life; he paid her off to keep quiet. His marriage had since ended so now the truth was coming out. She had done very well out of him and there never was a baby.

Now she was trying it on Nik. Maybe after she saw the photo of Nik and me she thought he would pay her off quietly to be rid of her. But somehow it hit the media first – maybe the attention excited her too. But she hadn't counted on him asking for a paternity test or wanting to do the right thing by her – I suspect she had a few problems. But most importantly, she admitted it wasn't Nik's child, and she wasn't even pregnant. She was going to be charged on several accounts for extortion, forgery and for false statements.

I put my phone down and turned to Nik; I snuggled next to him and laid my head on his chest, resting my arm across him. He was scarily silent. I wished I had a telepathic link to Ethan and he could tell me what to say.

Eventually he spoke. 'James said he and the Saints' lawyer got suspicious when she refused the paternity test. They got a hotshot investigator on to it and when they did some digging look what came up.'

'I'm sorry this happened to you Nik and to us,' I said. I regretted my actions but I did what I had to do at the time.

'It's just us again now, Süsse,' he said, breathing out.

'Yes. Where were we?' I asked, looking up at him.

'Wasn't I kissing you?' he teased and suddenly rolled me over, his tongue tickling me as I laughed and tried to beat him off.

*****

Alice and Kay were both so happy for me when I got to the office that it was ridiculous. The relief was palpable; it's the only way I can think to describe it. I heard the coffee van pull up and Alice and I grabbed Kay and Jim's orders and raced outside.

'For fuck's sake Russian, how did you beat me here today?' I looked at him two places ahead of me in the queue.

'Well Sasha,' he said, in a slow drawl. 'I just happened to be getting out of my car at the time when I saw the coffee van enter through the gates.' He pointed to them as if they were evidence.

'Whatever,' I said, and rolled my eyes. 'I give up!'

'Really?' he asked. 'How's the Kaiser?'

'Fine.'

'No really, how is he?' The Russian pushed.

'Well he hasn't been home since reuniting with Sasha if that tells you anything,' Alice piped up.

'That tells me a lot, thank you Alice,' he said, looking fondly at her.

I would have said 'whatever' again but two in a row might have been overkill. 'Consider him satisfied,' I said to The Russian knowing that would annoy him given he was currently single and probably didn't get any action last night. Surprisingly he was happy with the news.

'Sasha, I'm going to spot you a coffee today,' The Russian said magnanimously.

'Really?' I said, surprised and delighted.

'Really. What was that? A fat cappuccino?' he asked.

I smirked at him. 'A skinny latte.'

'Oh right, I'd get yours too Alice but I'm guessing you have other orders there and I'm not made of money.'

'Sadly true,' Alice said.

'You're a tight ass Russian,' I said. 'Your contract earns you more than all of us in this queue and you've got the security business as well. You should treat us all this morning just to be nice and because I helped the club out!'

'Fine then,' he said.

The queue line of eight staff cheered.

I rolled my eyes. I had managed to make him an accidental hero. Whatever!

The Russian stayed and paid for everyone's orders, bless him, and I waited with him, it was the least I could do and I wanted my coffee to be fresh and hot. As we spoke, I saw Lucas's Lamborghini coming through the gates. I knew the 'Captain onboard' alert would be going through the girl wires in the office. He smiled at me and gave Russian a wave as he entered the office. Fantastic scenery. Then my guy's car entered the grounds – we were both on a high this morning and could hardly tear ourselves away from each other. I grinned on seeing his car; I was pathetic really... such a pushover.

He got out of his VW and came over – what a vision he was in his white T-shirt and surf shorts, his board in the back. I could just lick that dried saltwater right off him. Where was I? Oh yeah, he came over and gave me a kiss in front of everyone and I didn't care. Can you believe it? Me either! But then again, I always was a bit of an idiot when it came to love, just check out my ex-husband. The Russian offered his hand and Nik shook it.

'Glad you're with us Kaiser, you would have upset me if you'd left,' The Russian said quietly as Nik's absence without leave wasn't public knowledge. It was so weird when The Russian was sincere, it always threw me.

'Sah-sha told me you motivated the lot of them into action, thanks Russian,' Nik said. 'Got to see Shayne but I need to see Sah-sha first,' he said, and waved a letter at me.

'Want a coffee? My treat today,' The Russian said.

'Yeah breakfast, thanks,' Nik said, and ordered a cappuccino. He pulled me aside.

'You're not serious? Don't tell me you haven't had breakfast yet,' I scolded him. Then I remembered the letter he was waving at me.

'What is it?' I looked up at him, concerned.

'Smile, it's good stuff,' he said, and I instantly relaxed. 'I sent that letter... the one to my father...' He said the words awkwardly. 'He wrote back.'

I felt my face light with excitement even though I tried to play it cool. 'And? What did he write back?'

Nik was smiling. 'He said he would love to meet me.'

I squealed and gave him a hug. The Russian called out from the coffee van. 'Cut that out you two or get in the car at least.'

I grimaced at him. 'I've never been a car girl, Russian,' I called back.

He raised an eyebrow. I turned back to Nik. 'This is wonderful, Nik, wonderful. Tell me what he said.'

'I'll tell you tonight, but it's promising,' he said, his eyes alive.

'Coffee's up,' The Russian called again. He was determined to annoy us and he hated not to be the center of attention. We gave each other a look that said so many things and returned to collect our coffees from the star of the coffee queue.

Chapter 27

That night after work and after Nik finished training, he came around again. I wasn't ready to send him back to his room at Alice's place just yet – we were still overcoming our pain and rediscovering ourselves, together.

I opened the door to him and breathed him in. He had showered at training and smelled fresh and divine. We kissed and held each other, drawing from each other and filling any remaining areas of doubt and pain. He saw the chair at the end of the catwalk and raised an eyebrow in my direction. I made him a coffee and led him to it.

'I'm hard just thinking about what this might be,' he growled in my ear.

'Behave and sit,' I ordered him with a smile. I ducked behind the screen I had set up at the end of the catwalk and sneaked a peek of him sitting there, sipping his coffee and waiting with anticipation. I put on my new Victoria's Secret underwear that he had bought for me and hadn't seen as yet – a faint pink satin, low cut bra and cheeky panties cut high on the butt cheek and framed with white lace. I slipped on two large, white-feathered angel's wings I had made – I bought the frame and when Nik was at training, I worked like crazy to get them finished. Then I put on my favorite jazz song – Cole Porter's *I've Got You Under My Skin* sung by Neneh Cherry – magic.

Nik looked up and smiled, loving it. He put his finished coffee cup down and waited, not taking his eyes off the catwalk. I turned the music up and appeared. He grinned and sat back, taking a deep breath and absorbing the scene as I walked down the catwalk as sassily as I could, turning occasionally, my wings in full flight, teasing him. He looked stoked as he leaned forward, his hands clenched between his legs, a grin on his very handsome face.

After coming close a few times, then turning around, I finally came to the end of the catwalk and he stood up and he picked me up, wings and all and whirled me around in a passionate kiss and embrace, landing me back on the catwalk.

'You take my breath away, a dream come true,' he said, undressing me with his eyes, and then he really began to undress me. I stopped him and, standing on the catwalk where I could almost look him in the eyes, I slowly removed his T-shirt, his track pants – allowing him to grab a condom from the pocket – and his boxer briefs, until I had his beautiful, toned form in front of me. He was lean, tanned and pure muscle.

He lifted me again and lowered me down onto the catwalk, wings and all. Healing sex was so wonderful and we were still experiencing it.

Nik kissed me slowly, moving from my lips to my neck. His reactions, his expressions were more naked than his body. 'I can't be without you, Sarsh, ever.'

'I love you, my guy. We won't let anyone separate us again.' I saw the flicker of a smile on his lips and relief flooded his eyes.

He slid my panties off and moved between my legs. He slid on the condom, and I wrapped my legs around his hips.

'You know, if it was you that was pregnant Sarsh, I would be so excited,' he said, honestly and openly.

'Maybe, one day.' I stroked his face.

'Definitely one day,' he said, not taking his eyes off me.

He moved faster, hungry, needing me and I loved it. I loved that he was not hiding how he felt – we were way past that. Lying on the hard timber of the catwalk, I felt him so deeply, he was so hard and my body clenched around him as if it refused to let him go. He groaned and I tensed with tightness and satisfaction.

Nik quickened his movements and we both panted heavily. I said his name once, twice, several times and his grip on me tightened. I cried out with pleasure and relief and pain.

Then we come in perfect unison, my back arching, Nik caving in to me, our breathing erratic and his face beautiful and desperate. I grasped him, my arms held him even though he was stronger and bigger, but I clung onto him anyway, hoping he would absorb my strength as I breathed in his.

We lay back, satisfied and relieved. I looked into Nik's eyes and he watched me and we said volumes in the silence.

*****

Eventually he spoke: 'I've just fucked an angel,' he teased.

'I'm sure that's a sin,' I told him as he helped me remove my wings and we moved to shower behind the smoky glass of my bathroom. Then, I fed him straight away – no nosebleeds or weight loss on my shift. While we ate, I asked him to share his father's letter.

Nik unfolded it and translated sentences for me: 'He said that he remembered my mother and that he had been selfish, stupid and irresponsible at that time of his life.'

I nodded. *Yep, men.*

Nik read my reaction and smiled knowingly. 'He said he would be proud and honored to meet me and to have a son.' He couldn't help smiling as he said the words. 'Can you believe it?'

'Yes,' I said, touching his face. 'Yes I can. I'm so glad you wrote,' I said, smiling at him.

'Me too. I wouldn't have done it if you hadn't encouraged me,' he said.

We finished our meal and moved to the sofa. I tangled my legs in his and asked Nik to read the letter to me from the top. He happily read it again. Nik's father had been married twenty years now and had four daughters. I laughed. 'He does want a son!'

He read on: 'he said they had tried for a son.' Nik grinned.

'And that his wife and his daughters would be delighted to meet me when I'm next home.'

I can't explain the look of happiness on his face, or what it must be like to be accepted. I was just so thrilled for him that tears welled in my eyes.

'I can't go back without you,' he said. 'They need to meet us both.'

'I'll be with you,' I assured him.

'Promise me?' he asked.

'I promise, I will be with you. In fact...' I thought about it, '...you might end up with a bigger family than mine.' I counted in my head. 'With my triplet brothers, Saffron, my parents, their budgerigar and Prada, it's eight to beat.'

Nik did the calculations. 'I might be one short, but if I can count you... or I could get a dog or a cat.' Just as he said it, Prada leaped from his lofty position onto Nik's shoulder and down to the ground, scratching him.

'Ouch, Prada.' Nik rubbed his shoulder. 'I wasn't going to get a dog, I was just joking.' He hurriedly looked at me. 'Don't say it.'

I grinned at him.

'We're not jinxed, we're special,' he said.

'Special?'

'Yes, special,' he said, and with that he pulled me onto his lap and began to kiss me just to prove it.

THE END

THE SAINTS TEAM SERIES
BOOK 4
TEAM
Alex
ALLY ADAMS

Team Alex:
Chapter 1

For just one moment I thought I was back in school and I had been pushed into the boys' toilet block – I remember the half a dozen faces that scowled at me, while I grappled with the smell, that huge water trough thing that we don't have in our toilets, and … well, I didn't stay around long enough to notice the other thing that we don't have, before tearing back outside to confront Susan Snowden, the bully that had pushed me in there. Fast forward about twenty years, and I'm almost in the same situation.

I'm due to record a quick interview in the Club Room with a player nicknamed Buzz – a Defender just back from injury and playing for the hottest sports team known to man, well, woman – the Saints. *Room Three*; I check the number, wander in and holy-naked-guys-getting-rub-downs … it appears I'm one of the few with clothes on.

Half a dozen faces turn and smile at me; I see a flash of glowing tight, tanned butts, muscly legs, toned arms, even a groin or two that was just 'out there'.

'Ah, sorry wrong room,' I say, as I stumble backward, trying not to look anywhere but out the door.

'Are you looking for the coach?' a voice from the corner booms.

I put my hands over my eyes, web my fingers a little which sets them off laughing again and look towards the voice. It was 'The Russian' – Alex Renwick.

'No, I'm after Buzz, he said to meet at this time in *Room Three*.' My face was burning red, but I think other parts of my body were enjoying it.

I could see several of the physical therapists shaking their head, smiling, and the youngest answered.

'It's his party trick. He thinks it's funny. Don't worry, you're not the first journo to fall victim.'

'I'll give him funny when I see him,' I muttered.

'Room eight, Carly,' the deep baritone voice said again. The Russian. He knew my name.

'Thank you,' I said, spinning on my heels to leave before I was magnetically drawn to that tall, dark, and gorgeous hunk of a man in the corner. Mm, The Russian.

*****

Yep, it was game day. Not my game day: my basketball team – the Suns – would have to go on without me, I was out of action with a knee injury, but I was reporting on the Saints' game day. Yep, the Saints – a tough gig but someone has got to do it.

After the interview with the very not-amusing Buzz, I settled into the media box, set up my laptop, made sure the WiFi was working and then stopped to look around. Sasha Saxon, the Saints' media officer, was walking towards me with two diet colas. She always grabbed them before the boys in the press box got them. Not that many of them wanted diet drinks, but we wanted them more ... it was our biological right. She looked super stylish as always with her gorgeous blonde hair tied back and her interpretation of the Saints' game day uniform.

'Hey Carly,' she said, sliding into the seat next to me. I noticed she said hello while keeping her eyes on the boys warming up on the ground – one boy in particular. A few months ago she had hitched up with Niklas Wagner, or the Kaiser as he is known – a truly beautiful specimen of German glory and the Saints' Midfielder. Mm. I watched her and laughed when she finally decided to give me her one hundred per cent attention.

She flushed. 'What? It's my job?'

'Sure it is,' I agreed. We greeted a couple of other journos who arrived in the box – Dan from radio *K-talk* and Brian from *The Sports Guide*. They grabbed desk space and began to set up their gear.

I had to ask Sasha something, and I wasn't looking forward to doing so. I looked around and lowered my voice ...

'Sash, I wanted to ask you a favor ...'

'Sure,' she said.

I cleared my throat. 'Next weekend I've got the Suns' Gala Ball and Auction Night ...'

Sasha frowned. 'Really? You're cutting that fine if you want a dress made.'

Sasha was a really good part-time designer when she wasn't working with the Saints.

'No, it's not that, but thanks,' I said.

'Well that should be fun,' she continued, 'especially if you're not organizing it. Or do you have to do something?'

'I've been asked to give a speech about the Suns and the importance of the team, given I played my hundredth game this year. Once that's over, I can relax,' I said, taking a sip of my diet cola.

'Right,' she said, and her eyes narrowed with suspicion. 'So, what's the favor?'

'I want to take a date.'

'Oh,' she looked surprised. 'I'm not your type, surely? I mean you're attractive, tall, nice legs, always admired your thick dark hair,' she said fingering a strand of her blonde hair, 'but ...'

I rolled my eyes. 'Not you, you dill,' I said, and she grinned. Funny girl! 'The Russian,' I said, lowering my voice.

She made one of those cringe-type faces.

'Why that face?' I frowned. 'I'm not asking him on a date-date, I need a handbag. He doesn't have to fall in love with me.'

Sasha shrugged. 'What's not to love ... he might fall head over heels. But rumor has it that his break-up with Leesa was ugly and he has sworn off women, for a while, anyway. But hey, if you're only after a bit of eye candy ...'

I nodded. 'That's all. Really tall eye candy.'

'I hear you. At least he's in town next weekend since we've got two home games in a row,' she mused. 'Why the Russian?'

I didn't want to let on that I had been lusting after him for a while now, so I played it cool and casual.

'I heard he was single, and he's taller than me which is pretty unique,' I answered.

She smiled at me. 'Ah, you saw him at the press conference earlier this season, I remember now. You asked me then was he single and I think he had just broken up with Leesa.'

I shrugged. The casual act wasn't working when my tongue was hanging out. 'So what's the story with his ex?' I didn't want to know but had to ask, couldn't help myself.

Sasha took a mouthful of her cola before answering. 'I only met her twice, sort of met her ... she came into the office once, and then I saw her at a home game here. She gave me a hard time because she wanted me to get The Russian out of the dressing room to speak to him before a game. As if!'

I laughed at the idea of pulling any professional athlete away from the team before a game unless it was super important. You are really in the zone before a game and the coach and captain would kill you if you went missing in action, especially if it was a LOVE call!

Sasha continued. 'She didn't like it here, too boring for her, not enough partying and stars around. You know, she's Leesa *Hart*,' she emphasized the surname. 'As in Harry Hart, the movie director's daughter?'

'Yeah, I vaguely remember some social media and pics going around at the time, although I was too focussed on getting through the season without an injury to really notice. Plus, no point noticing a guy who's hitched until they're unhitched,' I said, with a shrug.

We stopped for a moment to look out the media box window and watch the guys as they jogged past. Sasha sighed with contentment.

'Sorry where were we?' she asked. 'Oh yeah, The Russian and Leesa. I don't know how they ever got together, though. From what I saw and heard, you couldn't get two more complete opposites as those two. And she was always in the papers on the arm of some other guy, or at a party with a huge group of hanger-ons. It's lucky The Russian's mild-mannered, or he'd probably be in jail for murder.'

We both looked out at the Saints' stadium, contemplating relationships – well I was, can't really vouch for what was going on in Sasha's head.

'So,' she said, 'what do you want me to do? What's the favor?'

'Oh yeah, can you put me in his path?'

'That I can do. Can you drop into the office during the week? Come in to do a story, interview him or any of the team, take me for coffee, whatever excuse you'd like and I'll make sure you get one-on-one time,' she said, emphasizing the last few words in a sexy voice.

'What are you two nattering about?' Dan asked, butting in.

'First of all,' I said, rising and looking down on him – often the case with my height – we're not nattering, and secondly it's official girl talk.'

'I love girls' talk,' he said, with a smirk.

'Oh good,' Sasha said. 'I was just telling Carly that I was going to get a wax tomorrow. The Brazilian gets rid of those nasty little hairs ...'

Dan put his hand over his ears. 'Too much information,' he said, moving away.

Sasha grinned at me. 'Come in Monday if you can, he usually doesn't do much but drink coffee and mope around the office recovering from Saturday's game.'

'Thanks,' I said, relieved. The plan was falling into place and right on cue, The Russian ran right past our media box.

Hell yeah, he was definitely a man I could look up to – big, bigger than me ... I think he had a few inches on me; I might be able to get my high heels out ... yes! He needed a haircut, but he could get away with it ... his hair was full and wavy, dark and messy – cute. He had trendy stubble on his face as if he'd just gotten out of bed to come to the game. I couldn't see from afar, but I knew his eyes were dark brown with ridiculously long dark lashes for a guy – almost pretty, but I dare anyone to call him that. The Russian was strong - there was no better word for it. He liked to bench press; I liked him bench pressing too ... It was Sasha's turn to catch me out.

'Uh, don't forget to report on the game,' she whispered and gave me a wave as she departed the box.

I grinned and dismissed her, getting back to the job of setting up and reporting on the Saints versus the Salt Lake Spears. **To be continued...**

Order now as a paperback from: Amazon or as an ebook from Apple Books and Amazon.

Ally Adams is a journalist who lives in coastal Victoria, Australia, with her husband and furry friends. She is a literature major, romance reader and writer. Connect at:

Facebook: https://www.facebook.com/allyadamswriter
Website: https://www.allyadamsbooks.com/
Newsletter: Sign up for Ally's newsletter for latest releases, free chapters and beta reader requests.

Acknowledgments

Thank you to all the readers and bloggers who have loved Lucas, Tomás, Niklas, Alex, Mia, Alice, Sasha and Carly, and given me great encouragement to keep writing.

Special thanks to my German 'translator and sub-editor' who helped me with insider information – Becky Strahl. Catch Becky's blogspot at: http://inkeaters.blogspot.de/

Special thanks to the publishing team at Atlas Productions and Wild Hearts Romance for loving the Saints as much as me.

www.ingramcontent.com/pod-product-compliance
Lightning Source LLC
Chambersburg PA
CBHW031229120726
47905CB00002B/527